Books by Ed Dunlop

The Terrestria Chronicles
The Sword, the Ring, and the Parchment
The Quest for Seven Castles
The Search for Everyman
The Crown of Kuros
The Dragon's Egg
The Golden Lamps
The Great War

Jed Cartwright Adventure Series
The Midnight Escape
The Lost Gold Mine
The Comanche Raiders
The Lighthouse Mystery
The Desperate Slave
The Midnight Rustlers

The Young Refugees Series
Escape to Liechtenstein
The Search for the Silver Eagle
The Incredible Rescues

Sherlock Jones Detective Series
Sherlock Jones and the Assassination Plot
Sherlock Jones and the Willoughby Bank Robbery
Sherlock Jones and the Missing Diamond
Sherlock Jones and the Phantom Airplane
Sherlock Jones and the Hidden Coins
Sherlock Jones and the Odyssey Mystery

The 1,000-Mile Journey

The Search
for Everyman

THE TERRESTRIA CHRONICLES: BOOK THREE

*An allegory
by Ed Dunlop*

cross & crown
PUBLISHING
RINGGOLD, GEORGIA

www.dunlopministries.com
Cover Art by Laura Lea Sencabaugh and Wayne Coley

The search for Everyman : an allegory / by Ed Dunlop.
Dunlop, Ed.
[Ringgold, Ga.] : Cross and Crown Publishing, c2006
171 p. ; 22 cm.
Terrestria chronicles Bk. 3
Dewey Call # 813.54 ISBN 0978552326

It's a race against time as Prince Josiah, Princess Gilda,
and Prince Selwyn set out on a dangerous quest to deliver
the King's pardon to Adam Everyman in this third
adventure in the Terrestria Chronicles.

Dunlop, Ed.
Middle ages juvenile fiction.
Christian life juvenile fiction.
Allegories.
Fantasy

Second Edition
Printed and bound in the United States of America

Chapter One

A wispy tendril of gray smoke curled from the dark opening of the cave's mouth. It wafted across the clearing, pulsating and gyrating like a giant serpent slowly slithering through the air. Prince Josiah's heart pounded with the anticipation of danger as he dropped behind a large outcropping of rock.

"Aye, you were right," he whispered to his companion, Sir Faithful, who was just a pace or two behind him. "This is the dragon's lair! But how did you know?"

There was no answer.

Josiah turned. "Sir Faithful!" The castle steward was gone!

An angry roar rumbled from the darkness of the cavern. The ominous sound echoed across the clearing, growing louder and louder until it crescendoed down around the young prince like a deafening crash of thunder. As Josiah watched in astonishment, a strange light flickered inside the recesses of the cave and then a brilliant tongue of amber flame shot from the opening. The young prince trembled at the sight.

"Sir Faithful!" he whispered. "Sir Faithful! Where are you?" Prince Josiah hastily scanned the rocky hillside, but there was no sign of the kindly old man who had become his mentor and closest companion. Josiah was left to face the dragon alone.

A loud hiss and a thundering roar drew his attention back to the cave. He gasped in fright as a burst of flame more than fifty feet long shot from the cave. A fireball whistled through the air, struck a ledge of sandstone, and burst into a thousand fiery fragments that slowly drifted down toward the earth. The smell of burnt sulfur filled the air. At that moment, a huge green form exploded from the mouth of the cavern and burst into the sunshine. Josiah was face to face with an angry dragon more than thirty feet long! Inhaling sharply, the young prince dropped out of sight behind the boulder.

But he was too late—the dragon had spotted him. With footfalls that shook the earth, the huge beast rumbled heavily toward Josiah's hiding place, roaring fiercely and belching fire and smoke as it came. Josiah cowered in terror. A huge, scaly head with angry red eyes and a fearsome mouth appeared over the top of the rock. The mouth dropped open, and an ear-splitting roar made Josiah's head throb with pain. A blast of fire shot from the dragon's mouth, scorching the top of the rock and setting the nearby grass on fire.

Josiah rolled from behind the rock, leaped to his feet, and dashed across the clearing to drop behind another huge boulder.

The dragon spun around and lumbered toward the prince's new hiding place, snorting and roaring and breathing fire and smoke. The nauseating smell of burning sulfur grew stronger. Josiah coughed and struggled to breathe. The ground beneath him seemed to tremble with fear as the enraged dragon thundered closer.

The fire-breathing monster loomed over him. The scaly, serpentine tail lashed angrily from side to side. A blast of withering fire engulfed Josiah, scorching his face and singeing his throat and lungs. Noxious fumes filled the air. He gasped for breath. He fought against the darkness that threatened to swallow him up. "Sir Faithful!" he cried. "Help me!"

The dragon roared again. Huge wings beat the air as the dragon rose slowly and hovered at treetop level. A jet of flame stabbed the earth less than two paces from Josiah's foot.

My sword! the young prince thought frantically. *I must use my sword!* Rolling over with his back against the rock, Josiah reached inside his doublet for his invincible sword. His fingers closed around the book and he drew it hastily, swinging the volume with all his might and transforming it into a glittering weapon of steel. He leaped to his feet.

The dragon's head slammed into him at that instant, knocking him backwards and sending the sword tumbling harmlessly through the air to land in the grass behind him. "Sir Faithful!" Josiah cried in desperation. "Help me! Sir Faithful!"

He felt a crushing pressure as the immense mouth closed around his upper arm. The dragon had seized him in its teeth! The hillside seemed to fall away in a spinning, whirling confusion of motion and color as the fierce, fire-breathing monster lifted its head, snatching him high into the air. "Sir Faithful!" he screamed. "It has me!"

The furious dragon shook its head, jerking the young prince from side to side. Josiah felt as if his arm would be torn off. His body went limp, and darkness rolled over him in waves.

"Josiah! Wake up!"

Josiah slowly opened his eyes and cautiously raised his head. The dragon was gone. The fearsome, scaly head had been replaced by the grinning, freckled face of his friend, Prince Selwyn. "Josiah! Are you all right?"

"I—I think so," Josiah faltered. He waited anxiously, but as yet, could feel no waves of searing pain. Perhaps his injuries were so great that his mind was blocking out the pain. He blinked twice, trying to focus his eyes. Over his head, just beyond the face of his friend, he could see the branches of a eucalyptus tree. Just above that, the stone wall of a castle swam into focus. He turned his head. The beds of daffodils and hollyhock, the herb garden, the fountain—it was all so familiar. Suddenly he realized—he was in the east courtyard of the Castle of Faith. He shook his head in confusion. "How did I get here?"

Prince Selwyn stared down at him. "Get where?"

"How did I get back to the Castle of Faith?" Josiah asked, gathering the strength to sit up. His right arm ached. He gripped the flesh of his arm with the fingers of his left hand, squeezing gently and then summoning the courage to lift the sleeve of his jerkin and inspect the damage. To his surprise, there was no torn flesh. Not even a tooth mark. He couldn't believe his eyes. After the way the dragon had grabbed him and shaken him about, he had expected to find that his arm was badly mangled.

Selwyn laughed at him. "What were you dreaming about, Josiah? The way you were yelling and thrashing around, it must have been one exciting dream."

"Dream?" Josiah repeated. "I was dreaming? I was asleep?"

"I went to the armory to get a new bowstring, and when I came back you were stretched out on this bench, sound asleep. From the way it sounded, you must have been having one wild nightmare!"

Josiah rubbed his eyes and looked around, still not fully awake. "Then there wasn't a dragon." Part of him was relieved while another part was disappointed.

"Dragon?" Selwyn laughed again. "So you were fighting a dragon, were you?"

Josiah was embarrassed. "Well, actually, no. I'm afraid I wasn't doing much fighting. I dropped my sword, and I think where seven lustrous jewels glittered in the afternoon sunlight. "Sir Agape replaced the diamond for me. I lost nothing by helping you."

"Aye, but you didn't know at the time that he would do that," Prince Selwyn insisted. "You were willing to lose your diamond and forfeit the entire quest to help me."

"I only did what my King would have done."

Selwyn smiled. "I know. And I appreciate having a friend that was willing to sacrifice for me. Thank you, Josiah."

"Now that we have completed our quest," Josiah said, changing the subject, "what assignment do you think King Emmanuel will have for us? I am eager to serve him, aren't you?"

His friend's eyes grew wide. "Let's hope that it's something exciting. Something like killing a dragon and rescuing a princess." He reached within his own doublet and drew his sword. "I'm ready! Bring on the dragons!" The glittering blade slashed through the air.

Josiah laughed. "Your imagination is like a wild horse."

"What do you mean?"

"It's always running away with you."

Selwyn turned to him with a mock expression of hurt and betrayal. "And who was fighting dragons in his dreams a moment or two ago, may I ask? Just why should you have all the fun, my friend?"

"Aye, you can have the dragons. That dream wasn't much fun."

"Well, if you don't want dragons, then perhaps King Emmanuel will send us on a mission to storm a castle and recover it from the enemy."

Josiah laughed again. "Just the two of us?"

Selwyn shrugged. "Well, we would take some reinforcements. Just imagine—you leading one garrison of troops while I lead another." He raised his sword high in the air. "Forward, men!

the dragon was getting ready to eat me!" He rubbed his ey
again. "He had me by the arm and he jerked me way up int
the air and he was shaking me all around and..."

"That was I!" Selwyn was nearly doubled over with laughter.
"When I came down and saw that you were having a nightmare, I grabbed your arm and started shaking you. I was trying
to wake you up."

Josiah joined in the laughter. "I thought for sure that a fire-
breathing dragon had me and was ready to tear my arm off.
The smell of sulfur was so bad that I could hardly breathe." He
paused and looked teasingly at his friend. "It must have been
your breath."

"Thanks, my friend."

Josiah shook his head as if to clear his mind. "I'm just glad
that whole thing was just a dream. I was terrified!"

"If a dragon ever does grab you," Selwyn said quietly, "count
on me to come to your rescue. You know that I'd risk my life
for you, don't you?"

The two young princes had known each other for just a short
while, but already they were becoming close friends. Less than
a fortnight had passed since Josiah had found Selwyn dying
beside the highway on the way to the Castle of Charity, having
been assaulted and nearly killed by a band of robbers. Josiah
had saved his life and made a good friend in the process.

"I'll never forget what you did for me, Josiah," Selwyn said
softly.

"I only did what I knew King Emmanuel would have me
do."

"Aye, but you forfeited your diamond to hire the coachman
to take me to the castle. That was a very unselfish thing to
do."

Josiah turned his Shield of Faith and glanced at the face

Storm the walls in the name of King Emmanuel! Charge the gatehouse! The victory is ours!"

Josiah grabbed his arm and pulled the sword down. "Your imagination is running away with you again."

"Josiah, Selwyn, Sir Faithful is looking for you."

The boys turned at the sound of a pleasant voice to see a young girl hurrying across the courtyard. Slender and graceful, Princess Gilda was blond like her brother, Selwyn, and wore her long golden tresses in braids. A long, flowing gown of pale green satin and a shawl of exquisite white lace fluttered about her figure. As usual, her cheerful face was graced by a friendly smile of greeting.

"Your sister is every inch a princess, isn't she?" Josiah said softly. "Selwyn, she's beautiful."

His friend snorted. "Don't let her hear you say that," he growled, "or she'll become vain and haughty."

"Sir Faithful sent me to find you," Princess Gilda told the boys as she approached them. "He has an assignment for us."

Selwyn's eyes lit up with excitement. "I knew it! Josiah, this is it!" He held his sword high as he took a fighting stance. "We're going to fight a dragon!" Turning in Gilda's direction, he gave a slight bow. "Fear not, faint-hearted fair maiden. Prince Selwyn, at your service. My trusty sword will soon make mincemeat of yon dragon, and you will no longer live out your days in fear and trembling!"

The girl made a face and shook her head.

Josiah laughed and rolled his eyes as he looked in Princess Gilda's direction. "Your brother has a wild imagination."

She smiled sweetly. "Aye, he got that from our mother."

Selwyn held his sword against his side as she spoke, transforming the weapon into the book again and placing it carefully inside his doublet.

Josiah turned and started across the courtyard. "Where is Sir Faithful?"

Gilda hurried to catch up with him. "He was in the room beside the King's solar." She laughed in embarrassment. "It was on the second level, but I don't remember how to get there."

Josiah smiled. "I know where it is. Follow me. It does take a while to learn your way around the castle."

Prince Selwyn and his sister had taken up residence in the Castle of Faith just days before, having come from the Castle of Assurance. Although Selwyn was two years older than his friend, Prince Josiah had the dominant personality, and Selwyn had followed Josiah's leadership quite readily. Gilda, two years younger than her brother and almost exactly the same age as Josiah, had done the same.

"Sir Faithful seems like a really good man," the princess said as she fell in step beside Josiah. "He's so friendly and kind. I like him."

"Aye, he *is* a good man," Josiah said fervently. "He loves King Emmanuel with all his heart, and he lives solely for the purpose of serving him." His heart warmed as he talked about his friend. "Sir Faithful taught me to read, and he taught me the use of the sword, but most of all, he taught me about serving our King. He taught me to love His Majesty with all my heart. You won't find a more loyal friend than Sir Faithful."

He led the way up a flight of stone stairs. "He's the wisest man I ever met, so I go to him for advice whenever I have a problem. He always has time for me and he always listens."

They found Sir Faithful at a large oak desk with a quill pen in his hand. He looked up with a smile as the three young people entered the chamber and his clear blue eyes twinkled with warmth and genuine affection. "Well, if it isn't two of my favorite young knights! Princess Gilda, thank you for finding them for me."

Sir Faithful set his quill on the desk, stroked his long, white beard with the fingers of his right hand, and then picked up a scroll. "A message just arrived this morning from the Golden City of the Redeemed, my lords and my lady, and I think you'll find it particularly interesting, since it concerns the three of you."

Prince Josiah's eyes lit up with excitement. "Sire, does King Emmanuel have a mission for us? Prince Selwyn and I are eager to serve him. We'll go anywhere, do anything! Just give us an opportunity to serve our wonderful King."

Sir Faithful laughed at the youthful enthusiasm. He dropped his eyes and scanned the parchment in his hands. "Your King has placed a great deal of confidence in you, even though you are all so young. This message from His Majesty assigns the three of you to a very important mission. It won't be an easy assignment, and there will no doubt be some danger involved— but I know that you three are the right ones for the task."

"What is it?" Josiah asked eagerly. "Tell us—what is it?"

The old man smiled. "Give me just a moment and I'll tell you, Prince Josiah." He looked at Selwyn. "You haven't said a word, Prince Selwyn."

"I haven't had a chance to, sire," Selwyn replied, with a teasing look at Josiah. "Josiah hasn't given me a chance to get a word in. And in these past few days I've been around you long enough to learn that you aren't going to be hurried—it's best just to keep silent and let you speak."

Sir Faithful chuckled and looked at the parchment again. "This mission from your King is of the utmost importance. Somewhere in the land of Terrestria is a man by the name of Everyman—Adam Everyman. He's being held in a dungeon by

Argamor, and he has been condemned to be executed in just three weeks. King Emmanuel has issued Everyman a pardon. That's where you three come in—you are to find Everyman and deliver the King's pardon before the poor man is executed."

Josiah shuddered at these words, for his mind went back to the horrible days when he, too, had been held prisoner in a lonely dungeon by Argamor, the cruelest of taskmasters. It had been slightly more than a year ago that the Coach of Grace had come and Josiah had been set free by the nail-scarred hands of King Emmanuel. His heart went out to the condemned man. "Sire, where is this dungeon?" he asked. "How do we find Everyman?"

"Everyman is being held in an undisclosed location," Sir Faithful answered, reading the parchment. "Your mission is to locate the dungeon and deliver the pardon. But time is short, my lords and my lady, for the prisoner is to be executed in just three weeks. You must make haste. If you fail in this mission, this man will die."

Chapter Two

Prince Josiah, Prince Selwyn, and Princess Gilda stood speechless for several moments as the significance of Sir Faithful's words sank in. Josiah could hear the pounding of his own heart. Suddenly he felt completely overwhelmed by the magnitude of the mission to which he and his companions were being assigned by King Emmanuel. Suppose they couldn't find the condemned man in time?

He cleared his throat. "Sire, are—are you certain that the message was for us? There must be some mistake."

Sir Faithful shook his head. "King Emmanuel personally selected you, Gilda, and Selwyn. There's no mistake. His Majesty is placing great confidence in you to give such an assignment to ones so young." He sighed. "And it won't be an easy mission, I assure you. Argamor and his men will do everything in their power to stop you from delivering the pardon."

"Does—does Argamor know about this?" Prince Selwyn's voice came out as a nervous squeak, and Josiah suddenly realized that he was not the only one overwhelmed by the magnitude of the assignment.

"Aye, I'm afraid he does," the old steward said slowly. "He

has spies everywhere in Terrestria, and nothing escapes his attention. Rest assured, Argamor knows and will try to stop you."

Gilda spoke for the first time. "Sire, why is King Emmanuel sending us? What if we can't find Everyman in time? What if we fail to deliver the pardon?"

Sir Faithful raised his eyebrows. "This is indeed a very difficult mission," he told her. "But King Emmanuel chose you for a reason. He has confidence in you. Apparently, in all the kingdom of Terrestria, none is more suited for the task than you three." The old man smiled. "Go in faith, trusting King Emmanuel for the results."

A look of confidence spread across Gilda's pretty face. "When do we leave?"

"You must leave right away," Sir Faithful replied. "Today. There is no time to lose."

"But why us, sire?" Selwyn asked. "Why didn't King Emmanuel give this assignment to someone older? Someone with more experience?"

The old man carefully put the fingertips of both hands together before answering. "His Majesty has made the right choice. Youth are just as valuable in King Emmanuel's service as older folk. You and Prince Josiah have just returned from a pilgrimage of learning and growth and you were anxious to serve. King Emmanuel has given you an assignment—an important one. Why not throw yourself heart and soul into this quest and thereby honor the name of your King?"

"But sire, what if we fail? What if we don't find Everyman in time?"

"This is no time for fear and speculation of failure," the old steward replied. "You must leave immediately. The King's business requires haste. Never was that more true than right now. Don't worry about failure; simply obey His Majesty and carry out his assignment."

Josiah was feeling the same timidity. "Where will we look?"

"Everyman is in the Dungeon of Condemnation," Sir Faithful answered. "He—"

"I know where that is," Josiah interrupted. "It's in the Village of Despair. That's where Argamor held me prisoner for so long."

Sir Faithful shook his head. "This is a different dungeon, Prince Josiah. It is called by the same name, but it is in a different location."

"Then how do we find him, sire?"

"I would start by searching the Land of Unbelief," Sir Faithful said thoughtfully. "Undoubtedly that is where he is being held."

"Where is the Land of Unbelief?"

The castle steward rose from his desk. He turned and pointed to a large map on the wall. "This is a map of Terrestria." He touched a point on the map. "The Castle of Faith is right here on the north shore of the Sea of Conviction, just east of the Bay of Opportunity. If you travel two hundred forty furlongs due west across the Bay of Opportunity,"—he moved his finger across the map—"you will come to the Land of Unbelief. You ought to begin the search there."

Josiah moved close to the map and studied the region that Sir Faithful had indicated. The old steward placed his strong right hand on Josiah's shoulder and his left hand on Selwyn's. "Use caution, lads. The Land of Unbelief is a treacherous region with a vast, arid wasteland of skepticism and unbelief. It's a perilous place of dangerous quicksands, hazardous storms and ravenous predators that have claimed the life of many a knight. The land is inhabited by treacherous individuals who are not loyal to

King Emmanuel, and they will seek to do you harm. Argamor's forces will seek to oppose you and distract you and lead you into all sorts of temptations in order to keep you from delivering the pardon for His Majesty. This quest will not be an easy one."

Josiah felt uneasy. "Sire, what if we can't find Everyman?"

"Your book will guide you."

"But we've never done anything like this before. What if we say the wrong things?"

"Josiah, Josiah. All your King requires of you is that you simply deliver the news of the pardon. That's all."

"But what if we find Everyman and he won't listen to us? What if he won't receive the pardon?"

"The decision is Everyman's," Sir Faithful replied softly, "your assigned task is but to deliver the pardon."

"I'm not sure that I want to go," Gilda spoke up. "This is beginning to sound like a very dangerous mission."

"I'm afraid, too," her brother admitted.

"And I," Josiah said quietly.

Sir Faithful sadly shook his head. "My precious friends, your King has not given you the spirit of fear. He has given you the spirit of power, and of love, and of a sound mind. And remember, at any time during this mission you may send a petition to Emmanuel to request guidance or assistance. Go not in fear, but in the spirit of your King!"

He stepped to the door of the chamber and looked out at the sky. "Time is escaping like the falling grains of sand in an hourglass. You must make haste! The good ship *Obedience* is waiting at the postern gate to take you across the Bay of Opportunity. Provisions for your journey are already on board."

He glanced downward. "Are your feet shod with the preparation of the Gospel of peace? Good! Then there is not a moment to lose—you must set out on your mission immediately."

He thrust a rolled parchment into Josiah's hands. "Guard this with your life—it is the pardon for Everyman, which you must not fail to deliver. Remember, the man's life hangs in the balance!"

The three young people hesitantly followed the old steward to the postern gate, which was located on the southwest corner of the castle, guarded by a fortified gatehouse much like the main gate of the castle. The sentry raised the portcullis and opened the gate. Sir Faithful led the way down a protected walkway that led right down to the sea. A small boat bobbed gently in the swells at the foot of the walkway. Less than a furlong from the shore, a sleek sailing ship rode at anchor.

"You have the authority of His Majesty," Sir Faithful told them, "and no man may rightfully oppose you. There will be opposition, but you shall overcome it in the name of King Emmanuel. Captain Faithful Witness will take you across the sea to the Land of Unbelief where you shall search for Everyman. Go in faith, my princes and princess, and you shall honor the name of Emmanuel and return in victory."

Prince Josiah embraced the old man, and Princess Gilda and Prince Selwyn did the same. Without looking back at the castle they climbed bravely into the boat where a sailor was waiting at the oars. After a few moments of hard rowing, the small craft came alongside the ship *Obedience*. A rope ladder hung over the side. The sailor held the boat steady while the three young people climbed aboard the larger vessel.

"Welcome aboard!" a stout sea captain called, hurrying across the deck to greet them. "I am Captain Witness, and my crew and I will take you across the bay to the Land of Unbelief. The entire ship is at your disposal—make yourselves comfortable. We will get under way immediately."

The captain turned and called out a series of commands. The crew sprang to life, weighing the anchor and hoisting the sails. A brisk wind soon filled the billowing sails and the ship moved across the water at a rapid pace. The afternoon sun danced on the sapphire waters of the bay.

Josiah went to the bow and leaned over the rail, watching the breakers foaming against the forepart of the ship. Selwyn and Gilda joined him at the rail. "This happened mighty quickly, didn't it?" Selwyn said with a laugh. "It seems that just a moment ago I was wishing that King Emmanuel would send us on a mission— and suddenly here we are, sailing to a strange region to deliver a pardon to a man we've never even met!"

"I just hope we get there in time," Gilda worried aloud. "You heard what Sir Faithful said—Everyman will be executed in three weeks unless we can find him and deliver the pardon in time."

Josiah began to relax. "I'm thankful that King Emmanuel chose us to deliver the pardon. This is quite an honor."

"I too feel honored that His Majesty chose us for this assignment," the girl replied, "but I just hope that we can find Everyman in time."

With an energetic, bounding motion, the good ship *Obedience* surged eagerly through the sparkling waters of the Bay of Opportunity. High overhead, the huge sails were filled with a brisk wind, and the tall wooden masts creaked and groaned. The day was bright and sailing was pleasant. The three young messengers of King Emmanuel relaxed and began to enjoy the voyage.

"This doesn't look good!" Selwyn said abruptly. "There may be trouble ahead. Behold!"

Josiah glanced upward. The sky overhead was clear; the day was still sunny and bright. But to the west, far in the distance, a black line of forbidding storm clouds lay low on the horizon. As Josiah watched, the ominous thunderheads swept swiftly across the water like an advancing army of horsemen sweeping down upon a defenseless village. Lightning split the sky and thunder exploded with a vengeance. With a deafening roar that blotted out all other sound, a whirling black cloud swept down out of the heavens and touched the surface of the sea, drawing a swirling mass of water high into the air.

"It's a waterspout!" one sailor cried in fear. "We're all doomed!"

The wind struck at that instant, shrieking through the ship's rigging and instantly shredding the sails. The main mast snapped in two with a report that sounded like a crack of thunder. Sails, spars, and rigging came crashing down upon the deck. A huge wave slammed into the side of the ship and cascaded over the rail, soaking everything and everyone. The ship reeled and staggered like a drunken sailor.

"We're all going to die!" Princess Gilda wailed.

"The winds of adversity may blow," Captain Witness said quietly, "but the good ship *Obedience* can weather the storm."

Josiah stared in amazement. The captain stood calmly at the helm, gripping the ship's wheel in his strong hands. His chin was held high and the look on his face declared that he was almost enjoying the storm.

"Look, Captain!" a sailor cried.

Josiah turned, and the cold hand of fear gripped him. A frothy white wave taller than a mountain towered over the ship! The good ship *Obedience* rose to meet it, but the wave crested and broke, burying the vessel under countless tons of cold seawater. The young prince grabbed a stanchion and held on with all his might. His lungs screamed for air but he knew that if he lost his grip the surging waters would sweep him overboard to his death. With a strange slurping, gulping noise, the waters receded, and he gratefully gulped huge lungfuls of precious air.

"Josiah! Help me!" The scream cut through Josiah's preoccupation with his own perilous predicament. He turned to see Princess Gilda floating past, carried across the deck by the powerful currents. She was about to be swept overboard into the violence of the waves. "Help me, Josiah!"

Josiah released his hold, lunged forward, and managed to seize her by the wrist. The fingers of his other hand closed around a deck cleat, and he hung on for dear life against the surging water that threatened to hurl them both to their deaths in the depths. The *Obedience* suddenly rose through the water like a cork float bobbing to the surface as the water poured from her decks. Still clutching Gilda, Josiah rose to his feet.

"Oh, Josiah," Gilda sobbed. "You saved my life!"

Prince Selwyn appeared beside them. "I-I couldn't reach her, Josiah," he said quietly. "Thank you for saving my sister!"

The ship was still being pounded by the relentless waves. She tossed and reeled helplessly. The bow of the ship raised high in the air one moment, and then dropped with such force that Josiah felt sick at his stomach. The wind screamed in fury, hurling volumes of chilling seawater at them with a vengeance. The deck of the stricken ship was a confusion of tangled lines, broken fragments of mast and various items of ship's tackle. The three young people struggled across the deck, scrambling frantically over the debris, and managed to reach the companionway leading to the crew's quarters. They hurried inside, grateful to be alive.

"We're not going to make it, Josiah," Prince Selwyn said plaintively, wrapping his arms around his sister and drawing her close. "The ship is going to be broken to pieces! It will never survive the violence of this storm."

Josiah didn't answer.

In one incredible moment, the scream of the wind suddenly gave way to complete silence. The ship became as motionless as a rock. An unearthly silence prevailed. Captain Faithful Witness burst through the door. "The good ship *Obedience* has been sorely tested and tried, but she came through," he announced. "The storm is over."

The three young people followed him out onto the deck of the ship. The deck was littered with tangled lines, broken fragments of wood and various pieces of the ship's rigging, but she was still afloat. Josiah stared in amazement. There was no trace of the dark storm clouds that moments before had blackened the entire sky. The sun shone brightly in a cloudless sky and the surface of the sea was as calm as a millpond. The storm was over. Most amazing of all, the shore was less than a furlong away.

"Opposition will arise nearly every time that you undertake a great quest for King Emmanuel," Captain Witness told his wide-eyed young passengers, "but the good ship *Obedience* will take you through every time."

He pointed toward a narrow strip of sandy beach that bordered a dark, forbidding forest. "The Land of Unbelief," he announced. "My first mate will take you ashore in the longboat. May I wish you safety and success on your quest. We will make repairs to the ship while you are gone."

Ten minutes later, the longboat grated on the sand. Prince Josiah stepped timidly from the bow to be followed by Princess Gilda and Prince Selwyn. All three stood silently staring at the darkness of the forest before them. They were alone in a strange and hostile land, facing unknown dangers in their search for Everyman. Josiah suddenly felt very small and very much afraid.

Chapter Three

"What do we do now?" Prince Selwyn asked, speaking in a low voice as if he was fearful of betraying his presence by speaking aloud. The trees of the forest rose above them as strange and unfamiliar silhouettes, quite unlike any trees that Josiah, Gilda or Selwyn had ever seen. In the silver twilight of the approaching night they stood like hostile sentries guarding the perimeter of the forest against intruders. The young emissaries felt very vulnerable.

The lonely call of a bird floated across the silence, mournful and strange and eerie, and a cold chill went up Prince Josiah's back. He took a small step forward. "First we need to find shelter for the night," he suggested. "The darkness will be upon us before we know it."

As the young travelers neared the trees, Josiah realized just how enormous they were. Huge, twisted forms that rose hundreds of feet into the air, the massive trees towered over them, making the young prince and his companions feel as small as ants. Josiah took a deep breath and then let it out slowly. His heart pounded with fear.

The trio entered the forest, following a narrow path that ran up from the beach. The forest was dark and cold, with enormous hanging vines and huge, unusual plants unlike any that Josiah had ever seen. Grayish tufts of moss hung high overhead from dark branches slick with moisture. The atmosphere in the strange forest made Josiah uneasy. He turned to Gilda and Selwyn. "Stay close together," he said, whispering without realizing it. "This forest is unlike anything I have ever seen. There's no telling what sort of creatures inhabit a place like this."

"It's so dark in here," Princess Gilda whispered, looking around fearfully in the gloom of the forest. "How will we find our way?"

The two boys pulled their books from their doublets at the same instant. When they opened the volumes, the pages began to glow with a brilliant white light. Turning his book so that the light illuminated the footpath before him, Josiah led the way. A gentle rain began to fall on the dense canopy of trees overhead and within minutes the water was dripping down upon them with every step.

"We need to find a place of shelter," Selwyn suggested. "We're already soaked from our plunge into the sea, but this rain isn't helping anything."

"There," Josiah declared, holding his book high. "What do you think?"

They were standing at the edge of a small, mossy clearing ringed with tall trees. In the center of the clearing stood a cluster of giant toadstools which appeared as indistinct shadows in the dim light. The unusual fungi ranged in height from four to six feet, with caps that were bigger than the wheels on a farm wagon. Josiah, Gilda, and Selwyn scrambled under one of the shorter toadstools and huddled together for warmth.

"The parchment!" Josiah's heart sank. "Selwyn, I lost the

pardon for Everyman. It must have washed overboard when that huge wave struck the ship!"

"Are you sure?" his friend asked in dismay.

"I don't have it with me."

Discouragement descended upon Josiah, Selwyn, and Gilda as they realized that the precious pardon from King Emmanuel was missing. Without it, there was no point in continuing. "Maybe we should go back," Gilda suggested in a timid voice that quavered with emotion. The boys said nothing.

Night stole swiftly over the forest and it soon became so dark that they could scarcely see one another. An owl hooted nearby. Josiah shivered at the sound. "Maybe we should go back," Gilda said again. "Captain Faithful Witness said that they would stay and repair the ship, so the *Obedience* should still be moored in the bay."

"Aye, but we'd never find our way in the darkness," her brother retorted.

"We can't go back," Josiah said resolutely. "King Emmanuel sent us on this mission. He's counting on us to deliver the pardon! I won't fail my King."

"But we don't have the pardon," the princess argued, "so there's no point in going on. We've failed already."

"Listen!" Selwyn said urgently. The sound of twigs snapping told them that someone or something was coming down the path toward them.

Moments later they all heard an odd wheezing, scratching sound. Josiah held his breath as he waited to see what sort of creature was coming down the path. A pale green light glowed softly as it moved toward them with a fluid bobbing motion. When it came closer, the trio was amazed to see a huge, glowing caterpillar nearly three feet tall and more than twelve feet long! The unusual creature snorted and puffed as it resolutely wriggled its way through the dense forest.

The enormous caterpillar paused as it entered the clearing. The green glow illuminated the area and the young people could now see that the toadstools were a pale purplish color. The caterpillar raised the front portion of its body into the air and slowly swiveled from side to side as if it was searching for something. The creature's face was a hideous black mask that writhed and contorted continuously.

"It knows that we're here," Gilda whimpered softly. "It's looking for us!"

"Sh-h!" Josiah whispered.

The caterpillar shuffled closer and then raised up again and slowly turned from side to side. It did indeed appear to be searching for them. The three young people flattened themselves fearfully against the mossy ground.

After a few moments the enormous caterpillar turned and shuffled away, puffing and snorting as it went. The green glow faded from view when the unusual creature had passed. Selwyn let out a low whistle. "That is going to be one huge butterfly!"

"Hark!" Gilda said quietly. "Something else is coming!"

A pale green glow again illuminated the lower trunks of the gigantic trees. With the snapping of twigs and branches announcing its arrival, a second giant caterpillar entered the clearing. Just as the first had done, this one raised the front portion of its body off the ground and moved slowly from side to side as if it was searching for something. Moments later it moved away through the forest and the green light faded away.

"How many of these things are there?" Gilda whimpered. "They're so big and so... so horrid!"

At that moment a tremendous racket shattered the silence of the forest, startling the three young people. The sound was deafening. Josiah listened intently. The noise was so loud that it pounded painfully inside his head, but there was something strangely familiar about it.

"Behold!" Selwyn whispered. He had opened his book and in the light of its pages the three young people could see a gigantic cricket just beyond the cluster of toadstools. The huge insect's wings vibrated rapidly as a thunderous chirp reverberated through the forest. This cricket was a thousand times louder than any cricket that Josiah had ever heard.

"It's just a cricket," Josiah said.

"Aye, but it's almost four feet tall!" Gilda replied. "Oh, Selwyn, I'm afraid!" She huddled closer to her brother.

The night was long. The darkness was alive with strange clicks and buzzes and grunts and chirps and other bizarre sounds that struck fear into the hearts of the three royal visitors huddled beneath the toadstools. All throughout that long night the mossy clearing was visited countless times by gigantic, glowing caterpillars. They usually came singly, sometimes in groups of two or three or four, and each and every time Josiah, Selwyn and Gilda cowered in terror. Finally, the darkness gradually gave way to the light of morning.

"I didn't sleep once," Gilda said, crawling from beneath her toadstool hiding place and stretching. "Those scary noises kept me awake all night, and those horrid, horrid, caterpillars..." She shuddered, leaving the sentence unfinished.

Prince Josiah stood and stretched. He turned in a full circle, studying the little clearing in which he and his companions had spent the night. A thick mist hung just above the ground, giving the area an eerie, unearthly atmosphere. The toadstools now appeared powder blue in the pale light of morning. "Which way did we come?" Josiah asked. "I don't even see the trail."

"I don't know, but we need to head back to the ship," Selwyn said, appearing at his elbow just then. "Perhaps we can travel back to the Castle of Faith and somehow obtain another pardon for Everyman."

Josiah frowned. "Aye, but which way do we go? The trees are so thick that we cannot even see the sun, and I see no sign of the trail. How are we going to find our way back to the bay?"

Just then the ground shook violently beneath their feet, causing them to lose their balance and fall to their knees. Gilda sprang forward and grabbed her companions by the arms. Her eyes were wide with fright. "It's an earthquake!" she cried.

The earth shook again. "It's worse than that," Josiah replied. "It's a giant!"

The earth trembled and convulsed as the three travelers scrambled back under their toadstool. Their hearts pounded with fear. A huge boot suddenly crashed down through the branches at the edge of the clearing. Black and shiny with a huge silver buckle, the boot was more than twelve feet tall! Just above the boot was a huge green legging as thick as an oak tree. The smaller trees of the forest obscured the rest of the leg from view.

The boot swept upwards and disappeared from sight. Josiah leaned forward and peered from beneath the toadstool. Through a gap in the trees he saw a fearsome sight—a colossal, familiar face framed with red hair and a curly red beard. "It's th-the Giant of F-Fear!" he stammered. "But n-now he's ninety feet t-tall!"

A roar of rage shook the forest. "Who's trespassing on my land?" the giant cried. "I know that you're there! Come out and show yourselves!"

"W-what s-should we d-do?" Selwyn stammered.

"Stay hidden!" Josiah whispered. "If he finds us he'll lock us up as prisoners!"

"Beware!" Gilda screamed.

A huge thumb and fingers had suddenly appeared beside the toadstool. Josiah, Selwyn and Gilda dropped to the ground to avoid the grasping fingers. The cap of the toadstool abruptly disappeared as the giant hand plucked it from the stem, exposing the three terrified youth. "There you are!" the giant roared. "You can't hide from me!"

A huge hand reached for them, but Josiah was ready. With all his might he drove the blade of his sword into the huge thumb of the giant. A roar of pain shook the forest and the hand disappeared.

"Run!" Josiah shouted. Leaping to his feet he scrambled under another toadstool. Selwyn and Gilda were right behind him.

The cap of that toadstool disappeared as the Giant of Fear plucked it from the stem. The giant's face was contorted with rage. Cupping both hands, he pounced, but his intended quarry were already scrambling to other hiding places. "I'll catch you!" he screamed in fury. "You'll not escape me again!"

Josiah crouched beneath a dense thicket, breathing hard and trying to quiet his pounding heart. Remembering that the giant could not easily hear one so small, he called softly, "Selwyn! Gilda! Where are you?" *We've got to stay together,* he thought desperately. *If we get separated, we'll never find each other!*

"Josiah!" The young prince turned, and, to his immense relief, saw Selwyn scramble in beside him.

"Where's Gilda?"

"I don't know," Selwyn said with a look of anguish on his face. "I was hoping that she was with you."

Josiah turned. "Look!"

The Giant of Fear was down on his hands and knees, carefully parting the vegetation and searching diligently. Both boys knew immediately what he was seeking. "Josiah!" Selwyn whispered urgently, "we have to find her before he does!"

"Follow me," Josiah urged, and darted from beneath the thicket. The giant's back was to him, so he felt safe in dashing across the clearing to dart beneath a row of gigantic ferns that hugged the ground. Selwyn joined him.

"We have to find Gilda!" Selwyn said urgently. "Josiah, we have to find her!"

Josiah turned and faced his friend. He put both hands on Selwyn's shoulders and looked into his eyes. "We'll find her, Selwyn. We're not going anywhere without her. We'll find her."

"Come hither, tiny maiden," the Giant of Fear called suddenly. "You can't escape from me!" Still on his hands and knees, the giant leaned down until his face was just a few feet above the ground. Parting the dense vegetation with his huge hands, he flattened small trees and bushes as easily as a child would part a clump of grass.

"He's seen her, Josiah!" Selwyn cried. "Come on!"

The two young princes dashed through the woods as fast as they could. Josiah circled around to the side of the giant to avoid being spotted. Selwyn followed him. Josiah ducked behind a fallen log. "Gilda!" he called softly. "Gilda! Where are you?"

"The giant will hear you!" Selwyn warned.

"He can't hear us very well," Josiah replied. "We're too small."

"Gilda!" Selwyn called. "Gilda, we're coming!"

The boys moved closer. A huge hand swept over them, flattening the bushes around them and knocking the boys flat. Josiah rolled over and seized his sword, but the hand passed on. Apparently the giant hadn't seen them.

"Look!" Selwyn pointed. Ten paces away, a dense thicket trembled with movement. "It's Gilda! Come on!"

The two princes dashed forward and threw themselves beneath the thicket. "Gilda!" Selwyn called in greeting. "We thought you—" The words died in his throat. The disturbance in the thicket wasn't caused by his sister. The boys were face to face with one of the enormous caterpillars! The huge, repulsive creature wriggled toward them. The large mouth was rapidly opening and closing in the middle of the hideous black face. Selwyn was closest to the terrifying creature and he stood frozen with terror, unable to move.

"Run!" Josiah shouted. He scrambled to the edge of the thicket and then paused to check for the giant. Turning back, he saw that his friend was standing motionless, staring at the giant caterpillar. Selwyn's eyes were wide and his mouth was open, but he was paralyzed by fear, unable to move. The caterpillar wriggled closer, its black face writhing and contorting, its mouth still opening and closing rapidly.

"Selwyn! Run!" Josiah scrambled over and grabbed his friend by the arm, wrenching him away from the caterpillar, which now was less than two feet away. Selwyn fell backwards. He recovered his senses and scrambled to his feet. "Run, Selwyn!" Josiah urged.

"Josiah! Selwyn! Over here!" The boys turned to see Gilda waving frantically from beneath a nearby fallen tree. "Over here! It's a splendid place to hide." The trunk of the tree was nearly ten feet thick with a small ravine beneath it, creating the perfect hiding place.

The two boys dashed over and rolled into the ravine beneath the giant tree. Selwyn grabbed his sister and hugged her. "I thought the giant had gotten you," he teased, plainly relieved at being reunited with her. Gilda's eyes were wet with tears.

"What do we do now?" the young princess asked. "He's still searching for us!"

"We won't find a better hiding place than this," Josiah replied. "We'll just wait here until he gets tired of searching and decides to leave."

At that moment huge fingers closed around the trunk, whisking the enormous tree high into the air. "Run!" Josiah shouted, leaping to his feet and dashing toward the densest part of the forest in the hopes that the Giant of Fear would not be able to follow as quickly. Selwyn and Gilda were right on his heels.

The giant hurled the tree to one side and started after them. He tripped over his own feet and fell headlong, crashing to the earth with an impact that shook the forest.

The three terrified young people ran for their lives. The forest abruptly opened into a wide, unprotected meadow, but there was no time to choose a better course. Running as hard as they could, they dashed across it. Josiah looked over his shoulder just then to see a huge red head rise among the trees. The forest echoed with the giant's snarl of rage. "Selwyn! The giant is now hundreds of feet tall!"

"Josiah! Beware!"

Josiah turned just in time to stop himself from plunging headlong into a deep chasm that bordered the meadow. Standing on the very brink, he stared down into the rocky canyon. Far below, a raging river thundered furiously over jagged rocks, throwing white spray high into the air. There was no way across the chasm, and the Giant of Fear was right behind them. Josiah could see no escape.

Chapter Four

The Giant of Fear turned and spotted Gilda, Selwyn, and Josiah. With a roar of indignation, he raced across the meadow toward them. The ground shook with his every step. The three young people were terrified. Not knowing what else to do, Josiah drew his sword. *It's no use,* he told himself despairingly. *This sword is no match against such a giant! I might as well fight a lion with a needle!*

The angry giant tripped and fell just then, striking the earth with such force that acorns fell from nearby trees. He roared with pain and rage.

Josiah dashed toward a small clump of scraggly pine trees, the only hiding place that he could spot. "Selwyn! Gilda! This way!" The others followed.

"Prince Josiah!"

Josiah turned at the voice, and, to his amazement, saw a familiar figure standing at the brink of the chasm. "Sir Wisdom!"

The old man beckoned with his hand. "Come hither." The three terrified young people needed no second invitation.

"Help us!" Josiah gasped, as he and his companions reached the spot where Sir Wisdom stood. "The Giant of Fear is after us!"

Sir Wisdom shook his head sadly. "Josiah, Josiah. Where is your faith?"

"Do something, sire," the young prince begged. "Hide us! The giant is after us, and he's several hundred feet tall!"

The Giant of Fear had reached the edge of the meadow. Seeing his prey standing at the brink of the canyon, he calmly stalked toward them, confident that they could not escape. Gilda was trembling as she seized the sleeve of the old man's robe. "Save us, sire," she pleaded.

"Josiah, give me your sword," Sir Wisdom instructed. Josiah complied. The nobleman walked straight toward the Giant of Fear, raising the sword as he went. "You have no authority over these young ones!" he shouted. "They are servants to His Majesty, King Emmanuel, and I order you to harass them no more!"

"Stand aside, old man!" the Giant of Fear bellowed. "My quarrel is not with you."

"I order you to leave them alone!" Sir Wisdom shouted, still advancing fearlessly toward the towering giant. "You have no authority here."

"They are trespassing on my land," the giant thundered, but his voice carried a conciliatory tone, as if he felt obliged to explain his actions.

"This is King Emmanuel's land," Sir Wisdom retorted. "All of Terrestria is his domain."

"I have no quarrel with you, old man," the Giant of Fear declared. "Now, stand aside and let me have the trespassers," With these words he stepped forward. Stooping down, he reached a colossal hand toward the three cowering youth.

"Behold what faith and your sword can do!" Sir Wisdom said to Josiah. Leaping forward, he drove the steel blade of the invincible sword right through the giant's heart. A look of amazement and pain crossed the giant's face. Without a word, he toppled backward and fell to the earth. The impact shook the meadow.

"You killed him!" Gilda cried with joy. "The Giant of Fear is dead!"

Sir Wisdom handed the sword to Josiah. "He will live to trouble others yet, I am sure, but we have won the victory today."

"We thank you, sire," Selwyn said fervently. "You have saved the life of my friend and my sister, and mine as well. We are grateful."

Sir Wisdom smiled and turned to Josiah. "Why did you run from this ruffian?" he scolded. "Why did you not use your sword?"

"He was so tall," Josiah said lamely. "And he..." His voice trailed off.

"Then why did you not send a petition to Emmanuel? His Majesty always stands ready to help in time of need, my prince. As his child, you have the assurance that he will receive every petition that you send." The old nobleman sadly shook his head. "Josiah, I was greatly disappointed to see you and your companions running like frightened rabbits before this power-less buffoon."

"But—but did you see how big he was?" Prince Selwyn squeaked nervously. "Josiah was right—the Giant of Fear was several hundred feet tall."

Sir Wisdom turned toward him and gave a quiet snort of disgust. "Then why did you not send a petition to His Majesty? Enormous giants are child's play to him."

Selwyn shrugged, too embarrassed to speak.

"You do know how, do you not?" the old man queried kindly, stepping toward Selwyn. "My prince, you do know how to send a petition, do you not?"

"Certainly, sire," Selwyn responded quickly. "I simply write a message, roll it up, and release it. It reaches the Golden City in an instant."

"And King Emmanuel always receives the messages," Gilda chimed in. "He is always ready to help."

"The Giant of Fear has no authority over a child of King Emmanuel," the old man said sternly. "The next time he harasses you, claim victory over him in the name of your King."

"Of a truth, we will, sire," Josiah said meekly. He paused, almost afraid to voice the question that he had to ask. "What path do we follow to get back to the ship?"

Sir Wisdom stared at him. "Pray, why would you desire to go back to the ship?" he asked. "Prince Josiah, I know about the mission upon which His Majesty has sent you. You have not yet delivered the pardon to Everyman. Why would you leave without completing your assignment?"

"We have lost the King's parchment," Prince Selwyn said quietly, coming to Josiah's defense. "We cannot deliver the pardon to Everyman, for we no longer have it."

"If we can get back to the ship, perhaps we can go back to the Castle of Faith and get another pardon from King Emmanuel," Gilda spoke up. "But we do not even know in which direction the Bay of Opportunity lies, or how to find the ship."

"We have failed our King already," Josiah finished, hanging his head.

The old man smiled. "You have not failed your King," he reassured them gently, looking from one young person to another. "You have not lost the pardon." He extended a hand to Josiah. "Give me your book." Josiah reached within his doublet and withdrew his book, a bit perplexed as he handed it to the old man. "King Emmanuel's pardon for Everyman is found within the pages of your book," Sir Wisdom told Josiah, opening the volume to the back. He held up a parchment, which was sealed with the royal seal of King Emmanuel. "Behold the King's pardon."

The three young people immediately felt a tremendous sense of relief. "Then we can continue with our mission," Josiah declared.

Sir Wisdom replaced the precious document within the pages of the book. Closing the volume, he handed it back to the young prince. "The King's pardon is always found within the pages of your book."

He gestured across the mighty chasm stretching before them. "This is the River of Timidity," he told them. "The Land of Unbelief lies on the far side. To reach the dungeon where Everyman is held, you must cross this river."

"But how can we do that?" Prince Josiah asked in astonishment. "I see no way across."

"Step across it," the old man replied, with a slight smile. "How else?"

"What?" Josiah searched Sir Wisdom's face, trying to determine whether or not the old man was jesting. "But sire, the chasm is at least a furlong across!"

"It is not as large or as difficult as you perceive it to be." Sir Wisdom turned to Prince Selwyn and Princess Gilda. "Can you not step across it?"

The brother and sister both shook their heads. "I don't think so, sire," Selwyn said slowly. "As my friend Josiah has said, sire, the chasm is at least a furlong across. No man in Terrestria could hope to leap over that."

"The River of Timidity must be crossed by any messenger from the King who will take a pardon to the inhabitants of the Land of Unbelief. For some, the crossing is very easy. Others falter and turn back when they reach this chasm, but the crossing is not as difficult as it would seem at first. Any child of the King may cross it with a simple step of faith."

"But, sire, that's impossible!" The words were out before Josiah could stop them.

Sir Wisdom turned to him. "Do you trust me, Josiah?"

"Aye, sire, but—"

"Have I ever lied to you?"

"Nay, sire."

"Would I ever lead you astray, or do anything to harm you, or cause you to dishonor the name of your King?"

"Nay, sire."

"Then do as I say, my prince. The River of Timidity must be crossed, or the pardon from King Emmanuel will never reach Everyman in time. Simply step across the chasm. It is not as difficult as you might think."

"But, sire—"

"Trust me, Josiah. I speak for King Emmanuel. Step across the chasm."

Josiah stepped to the very brink of the perilous chasm. His heart pounded with fear. His legs grew weak and began to tremble. He struggled to draw a breath.

"Simply step across, my prince."

Taking a deep breath, the young prince stepped forward. He looked down, and to his utter astonishment, saw that he was stepping across a tiny furrow, at the bottom of which was a tiny trickle of water! In an instant he was standing safely on the opposite side.

"Are you all right?" Gilda stood at the edge of the little crevice, leaning forward and cupping her hands to her mouth as she shouted, though Josiah was standing barely a pace away.

"Aye, I'm all right," Josiah replied in a quiet voice. "Come on across."

"What?" Gilda shouted.

"Come on across," Josiah repeated. "It's easy, and there is no need for fear."

"I'm afraid!" Gilda shouted.

Josiah laughed. Could she not see that one small step would take her across the tiny rivulet of water? What was there to be afraid of?

"Step across, my child," Sir Wisdom admonished her. "There is no need to fear."

"Let my brother go first," Gilda begged. "He's the oldest, anyway."

"That would be appropriate, would it not?" the old man agreed. "An older brother setting the example of faith for his little sister. Prince Selwyn, why don't you go next?"

Selwyn paled, but he stepped to the edge of the tiny ditch, eyeing it with apprehension written across his face. He hesitated, glanced across at Josiah, and then shook his head. "I—I can't," he faltered. "I just can't."

"Trust me," Sir Wisdom said gently. "I have served King Emmanuel faithfully for many generations, and I would never lead one of his children astray. The River of Timidity must be crossed if the pardon is to reach Everyman in time. Your King would not have sent you upon this assignment unless he knew that you would be successful. He will never lay upon one of his children any burden that is too great to bear. Prince Selwyn, trust your King and simply step in faith across the chasm."

Selwyn hesitated for a moment, glanced across at Josiah, and then stepped across the tiny rivulet. Josiah saw the look of fear upon his face change instantly to one of utter astonishment.

After seeing the two boys cross successfully, Princess Gilda stepped to the edge of the chasm and without hesitation stepped across the River of Timidity. She immediately turned and stared down at the tiny streamlet of water. "It's just a little trickle!" she exclaimed in astonishment. She turned to Sir Wisdom, who had stepped across to join them. "But why did it appear to be so huge a moment ago? It was a tremendous canyon."

"There are obstacles in the path of anyone who will serve King Emmanuel," the old man replied quietly. "Fear will magnify any obstacle, making it seem far larger than it really is. That's why the tiny stream called the River of Timidity appeared to be a raging torrent at the bottom of a hazardous canyon. But when one steps out in faith and obedience to the King, the obstacles become small and insignificant."

He gestured toward a narrow path that led through the woods. "Follow this path, for it will lead you right into the heart of the Land of Unbelief. It is there that you must begin your search for Everyman. Be careful to guard your own hearts for the King, lest the unbelief of this impoverished land should influence you. Take care that you do not wander into the Valley of Indifference, for it is perhaps the most treacherous place of all. The poisonous vapors from the swamps in that region produce a lethargy that is deadly to a child of the King."

The forest before them was dense and foreboding, filled with ominous shadows and dark, indistinct forms. Anxious to show that she was unafraid, Princess Gilda hurried ahead around a bend in the trail. Seconds later her scream of terror filled the air. Josiah felt his own heart constrict with fear.

Gilda's face was white as she darted back around the bend. She ran to Sir Wisdom and seized both of the old man's hands. "It's one of those horrid caterpillars!" she wailed. "It's coming this way! Help us, sire!"

At that moment a huge caterpillar wriggled into view with the curious humping motion peculiar to such creatures. The enormous beast's baggy skin was pale green with streaks of soft yellow and sagged in great folds and wrinkles like a garment three sizes too large. Fine, silvery hair several inches long covered most of the huge body, sparkling and glistening in the bright morning sun. The caterpillar's hideous black face writhed and contorted and its mouth opened and closed repeatedly. As the three young people watched in dismay, the caterpillar wriggled up to Sir Wisdom, raised the upper portion of its body into the air, and proceeded to wriggle from side to side as it rubbed its ugly head against the old man's shoulder.

"Leidra, old girl, how are you?" Sir Wisdom asked, gently stroking the head of the unusual creature with both hands.

The three young people stared in bewilderment. "Do you—do you know this caterpillar?" Gilda asked in amazement. "You were talking to it."

"This is Leidra," the old man replied. "She's an avral. They're quite friendly to humans, and can be very helpful in times of distress." He beckoned with one hand to Gilda. "Come, my dear, stroke Leidra's face for her. Avrals love to be touched."

Gilda drew back. "I—I can't," she faltered.

"She won't hurt you," Sir Wisdom said gently. "She and her kindred have been searching for you, in order to guide you across the badlands."

"They—they want to help us?" Josiah blurted.

"They're really very helpful creatures," the old man explained, "and they take great delight in being with humans."

Josiah stepped closer. Reaching out timidly, he touched the black face of the avral, finding that the creature's flesh was at the same time both firm and soft to the touch. The avral's face writhed and contorted furiously. The mouth opened and closed erratically. Josiah drew back. "Did I hurt her?"

"Nay, nay," the old man replied with a chuckle. "That's her way of showing her delight at having you stroke her. She likes you."

Josiah dropped his hands down on the avral's body and began to stroke the fine silver hair, finding it extremely soft and silky to the touch. The huge creature wriggled with delight. Its face distorted and twisted even more rapidly. "This is incredible!" Josiah breathed. He vigorously stroked and petted the soft, silky body. Leidra responded by raising her upper body in the air and pressing against Josiah, like a dog jumping up to lick its master's face. Instead of revulsion, the young prince felt a sense of wonderment and delight.

"She trusts you, Josiah," Sir Wisdom told him, beaming with approval. "Avrals love to be with humans, but they usually don't take to a stranger as readily as she has to you. She likes you."

Selwyn stepped close and began to pet the giant caterpillar, and before long, Gilda was doing the same. "She's so soft," the young princess remarked. "Her hair is like silk."

"I must leave you," the old man told them, "but Leidra will accompany you across the badlands. Simply tell her where you want to go, and she will take you there. You can trust her implicitly."

"Do avrals understand English?" Josiah asked in astonishment.

"They understand almost everything you say," Sir Wisdom replied. "They're very intelligent creatures, and, as I said, very helpful and affectionate. Leidra will be a great help in your search for Everyman."

Gilda stepped in front of the great caterpillar and placed her hands on each side of the ugly, rubbery face. "I'm sorry for what I said about you, Leidra," she said quietly. "I was afraid of you, for I had never seen an avral before last night. You really are quite nice; you really are. I hope we can be friends."

Leidra's face wriggled furiously. She leaned against Gilda. Sir Wisdom laughed. "I think she accepted your apology, Gilda."

He glanced skyward to check the position of the sun. "Well, I really must be hurrying along. Go trusting in your King, and you shall find success in your mission. Leidra will assist you."

"Wait, sire," Prince Selwyn said. "I have a question. Do avrals become big butterflies or moths?"

"Avrals are the larva stage of huge butterfly-like creatures called lepidopteras," the old man answered. "Lepidopteras have thirty-foot wingspans with the most dazzling, iridescent colors that you can imagine. They're the most magnificent creatures in all of Terrestria! Leidra is relatively young, as avrals go. I think she's a little less than three hundred years old, so she won't change into a lepidoptera for another two or three hundred years."

Sir Wisdom embraced each of them briefly. "Farewell, my young friends. I wish you every success in your mission for our King. You must make haste, for Everyman does not have much time left. If the King's pardon does not reach him in time, he will perish. You must make haste." With these words, the old man gave the avral an affectionate pat and then hurried off through the forest.

"Which way do we go?" Selwyn asked, looking about in the gloom of the forest. "There doesn't seem to be any sort of a trail."

Josiah moved forward and stepped in front of the avral, which immediately raised the front half of her body into the air. The young prince reached up and stroked her face. "Can you show us the way, Leidra?" he asked. "We have to find Everyman, but we don't know the way."

Leidra dropped to the ground and shuffled forward through the undergrowth. "Come on," Josiah called to his companions, "I think she's showing us the way!" Gilda and Selwyn fell in behind him and they began to follow her single file.

The avral scurried forward at such a brisk pace that the three young people had to hurry to keep up with her. Turning neither to the right nor the left, the huge caterpillar led them in a straight line through the forest, crashing through brambles and thickets, climbing over fallen logs, scrambling through ravines and gullies. Never varying one inch from her course, Leidra turned aside for nothing. Josiah waited to see what would happen when she encountered one of the mammoth trees, but to his amazement, the route that the avral had chosen passed between the trees without running up against any of them.

After twenty minutes of traveling at a brisk pace, the travelers left the forest behind. Leidra topped a small rise and then came to an abrupt stop. Huffing and puffing as they caught up with her, Josiah, Selwyn, and Gilda stared in amazement at the scene that met their eyes.

They found themselves standing at the brink of a gentle valley that looked as if it were made from transparent blue glass. The hillside on which they were standing fell away below them in a series of gentle ridges that shimmered and glistened with a strange blue light. There was no vegetation of any kind in the valley. Buttes and mesas and strange formations rose before them in the center of the valley, and all were made of the same glistening, transparent blue material.

"It's a valley of glass," Gilda breathed softly. "How beautiful." She pointed. "Look, you can see the reflections of the clouds!"

Josiah stepped around Leidra. As his boots touched the transparent blue material, his feet shot out from under him without warning. He found himself sliding headfirst down the slick incline. It happened so quickly that he didn't even have time to cry out.

Chapter Five

Prince Josiah's heart raced as he plunged helplessly down the slippery slope. He picked up speed, sliding faster and faster and faster until his surroundings melted into a pale, indistinct blue. He reached out with both hands in an attempt to slow his descent, but the slope was as slick as wet ice and his frantic struggles found no handholds. Drawing his arms and legs close to his body, he curled up into a ball and waited.

He was abruptly thrown sideways, spun about, and catapulted back in the opposite direction. Moments later he found himself spinning dizzily round and round on his back. The blue world around him slowed to a gentle stop. He looked around. He was lying in a large depression of blue glass—or ice or crystal or whatever it was—about fifty feet across. Above him rose several shapeless projections of the transparent blue material. Apparently, they had halted his unexpected slide into the valley of glass. He rose shakily to his feet, but the basin was as slick as the rest of the valley, and his feet shot out from under him again.

"Josiah!" A tumbling, spinning form shot past him, careened wildly up the smooth face of one of the formations, and then plunged straight back at him. He rolled out of the way in the nick of time. As the whirling body slowed to a stop, Josiah saw that it was Gilda. Afraid to stand, he crawled carefully toward her.

"Josiah! Are you all right?" She tried to stand and fell flat.

"Don't try to stand up," Josiah cautioned. "It's too slick. Are you hurt?"

"I think I'm all right," she assured him. "Are you?"

"I'm fine," he told her. He looked back up the slope in the direction from which he thought he had fallen. "Where's Selwyn?"

"I—I don't know," she replied, biting her lip. "When you fell we both stepped forward and fell at the same time. I thought he'd be down here, too."

"I'm right here," Selwyn's voice called, and they both turned to see him crawling carefully across the basin toward them. "How do we get out of here?"

"I don't know," Josiah replied, rising up on his knees and glancing around. "This stuff is as slick as glass!"

"It *is* glass," Gilda said.

"We don't know what it is, but it is slick," Josiah told her. "Don't try to stand up—you'll just fall down again."

"But how do we get out of here?" Selwyn asked again. "We'll never climb back up that slope."

Gilda pointed. "Look."

The boys looked in the direction that she indicated and to their delight saw Leidra making her way down the slope toward them. The avral was gliding toward them with the same humping, wriggling motion that she used in the forest. The slippery slope seemed to cause her no difficulty whatever. "She can walk on glass!" Gilda cried.

The giant caterpillar came to a stop in front of the three young people and raised up in the air as if to greet them. Gilda crawled forward, and, gripping the avral's fur, pulled herself to a standing position. "Leidra, are we glad to see you!"

"What is she doing?" Selwyn asked. The avral twisted her head around to one side and touched her back. Jerking back and forth, she repeated the motion several times.

"I think she wants us to climb on her back!" Josiah cried. "Perhaps she can carry us out of here."

Gripping the avral's silvery hair, Gilda managed to clamber up onto Leidra's back. The creature's rubbery face writhed and contorted and Josiah recognized the movements as a sign of pleasure. "That's what she wanted," he said. In no time, the two young princes were seated behind the girl, and the avral started forward.

"It's like riding a horse made of silk," Josiah commented, as Leidra carried them swiftly across the slick contours of the glass valley. "She's softer than any saddle, and her movements are smoother than any horse."

Gilda laughed. "This is like riding a horse and riding an ocean wave at the same time. Every few seconds it feels as if a wave is passing under us." The wave of gentle motion passed beneath the three riders just then, lifting them two or three feet higher and then lightly lowering them again.

"Up and down, up and down," Selwyn remarked. "It really does feel like we're bobbing about in the water, doesn't it?"

Leidra came to a steep incline, but the slippery slope proved to be no problem for her and she climbed it effortlessly. Gripping her silky fur, her three passengers hung on tighter than ever and somehow managed to keep their seats. "We would never have made it out of here without Leidra," Josiah told the others.

The avral topped the incline and started down into a steep hollow. Josiah grasped Leidra's fur with one hand and leaned down to touch the glassy surface upon which the giant caterpillar traveled so effortlessly. He marveled at the ease with which the avral moved.

Gilda pointed. "Look."

Josiah leaned to one side to see around Selwyn and Gilda. A peasant man and woman were down upon their knees in the bottom of the slick ravine, clawing at the blue glass of the wall above them in a vain attempt to climb out of the valley. "We can help them," Gilda suggested. "Leidra can carry them, too, I'm sure."

"We're here to help you," Selwyn called to the two peasants as the avral approached the point where they struggled so helplessly. "Climb on."

"We don't need your help," the man answered gruffly, never pausing in his attempt to climb the glassy wall. "We're doing just fine on our own."

The woman turned and glared at them. "Do you think that you're better than we are? Why do you condemn us? Why do you look down on us? We're just as good as you are."

"We're not trying to condemn you," Josiah replied. "We're trying to help you. The valley is slick, and the walls are too steep to climb, but the avral can climb them easily. She can have you out in no time."

"We told you that we don't need your help," the man growled. "Now why don't you just go away and leave us alone?"

Leidra moved on, leaving the peasants to their futile struggles. Josiah looked back and watched them for a moment, shaking his head in sorrow. The man and woman would never make it out of the glass valley on their own, but they were too proud to admit that they needed help.

Less than fifteen minutes later, Leidra had reached the far side of the glass valley. As she topped a small rise, the three young people could see a wilderness area with gently rolling hills and bright meadows. A narrow trail led across a small clearing and disappeared over the crest of a grassy hill adorned with colorful splashes of wildflowers. The avral scurried across to the trail and then stopped when she reached it.

"What is she waiting for?" Princess Gilda asked impatiently. "Come on, Leidra, let's go!"

"I'm afraid this is the end of our ride," Prince Josiah told her. "I think she wants us to get down."

The three young people scrambled down from their comfortable perches on the back of the avral. "It's back to walking," Prince Selwyn said with a sigh. "This was a great way to travel."

Leidra raised her upper body and rubbed her head against Josiah's shoulder as if to say good-bye. She did the same with Gilda, and then with Selwyn. After saying her farewells, the giant caterpillar glided across the meadow to join two other avrals that were feeding on the lower branches of the trees bordering the clearing. "I'll miss you, Leidra," Gilda called softly. "I'm sorry for what I said about you and all the other avrals; for I had never met an avral before." She wiped at her eyes with the back of her hand.

Watching Leidra wriggle across the meadow, Prince Josiah felt a haunting sense of loss. He would miss the enormous, gentle creature. In spite of her frightening appearance, the giant caterpillar had been a tremendous help to the young prince and his companions.

"Where do we go from here?" Selwyn asked.

"I suppose that we just follow the trail until we come to a town or village to ask directions," Josiah replied.

"Perhaps we should send a petition to King Emmanuel," Gilda suggested.

Josiah nodded. "Indeed we should. Our mission to deliver the pardon to Everyman will end in failure unless we have Emmanuel's help and guidance." He took a parchment from his book and wrote a brief message to Emmanuel.

"*To His Majesty, King Emmanuel:*
We have entered the Land of Unbelief in search of Everyman that we might deliver your pardon to him. We humbly ask for your guidance and that you would grant us success in our mission for you. Keep us safe from harm.

Your children, Prince Selwyn, Princess Gilda, and Prince Josiah."

Josiah rolled the parchment tightly and then released it. All three watched in silence as the petition shot from the young prince's hand and disappeared over the trees. "It's still so amazing, isn't it," Gilda remarked softly, "to think that we can communicate with King Emmanuel in an instant, no matter where we are!"

"The thing that thrills me," Selwyn replied quietly, "is that His Majesty always receives our petitions simply because we are his children."

Josiah smiled, for he had been thinking the very same thing.

The three young people started down the trail at a brisk pace. "If this is the Land of Unbelief," Gilda said a moment later, "are we in any danger? I have heard of this land, and it seems that it was always spoken of as a place of peril and danger. And Sir Faithful warned us that it was a land of quick-sands and storms and people who would try to hurt us."

"I would not choose to come here," Josiah replied, "were we not on a mission for King Emmanuel. If we go trusting in our King, I believe that we shall be safe from harm, even in the Land of Unbelief."

"Sir Wisdom told us to guard our hearts," Selwyn said,

turning to look over his shoulder, for he was in the lead. "He said that the unbelief of this land can influence us if we are not careful."

Josiah paused in the middle of the trail. Using his sword, he cut a stout staff to use as a walking stick. When Selwyn and Gilda admired his, he cut two more walking sticks. The three royal visitors continued their journey.

"We must be careful," Josiah agreed, resuming the conversation from a moment before. He swung his staff at a leafy branch hanging over the trail. "The Land of Unbelief is a perilous place, but it is here that we will find Everyman."

"What will happen to him if we do not find him in time?" Gilda worried.

"Everyman is a condemned man," Josiah replied soberly. "If we fail to deliver King Emmanuel's pardon in time, I suppose that he will be hanged."

The young princess shuddered. "We must hurry," she declared. "We must find him before it is too late!"

The boys both nodded in agreement.

Josiah had never met Everyman, but in his imagination he could almost see the condemned man languishing in his cold, dreary cell. He could imagine the look of terror that passed across the man's face as he heard the tramp of the guards' feet on the stone floor of the dungeon corridor. He could almost see the leering grins on the faces of the cruel guards as they unlocked the door. "Come, Everyman," they would say, "Your time is up. The time has come for your walk to the gallows."

"No!" Josiah shouted aloud, and his companions both looked at him in alarm. "We must not allow that to happen! Everyman has been pardoned. He has been set free by the King's decree. We must not allow him to perish. We must reach him with the pardon!"

Selwyn grasped Josiah's elbow. "We'll reach him in time, Josiah," he said quietly. "We must."

Josiah looked up and the prison scene vanished. "I'm sorry," he said sheepishly. "I was imagining the dungeon where Everyman is being held, and I could see the guards coming to take him to the gallows, and..." His voice faltered. "We have to reach him in time, Selwyn. We must!"

"We will, Josiah. We will."

Two hours later the trio came to a fork in the trail. "Which way should we go?" called Gilda, hiking along five or ten paces ahead of the two young princes. "Both trails look the same."

Josiah paused when he reached Gilda and reached within his doublet for his book, but at the same moment he spotted a woodcutter hiking up the trail toward them. The man was dressed in homespun and carried a sharp, double-bladed axe over his shoulder. "Sire," Josiah called, forgetting his book for the moment, "are you a resident of this land? Do you know this region?"

"Indeed I am, my lord, and indeed I do. How may I be of assistance to my lords?" He gave a slight bow in Gilda's direction. "And, of course, to my lady."

"We're looking for the Dungeon of Condemnation," the young prince told the woodcutter. "We have a pardon from King Emmanuel for a prisoner who is called by the name of Everyman."

"The Dungeon of Condemnation," the woodcutter mumbled. "A pardon from the King. Hmm-mm. Aye, my lord, I can direct you there." He turned and pointed down the pathway to the left. "This trail will take you through the Valley of Unfortunate Mistakes. Follow the trail, for it will lead you to the dungeon of which you speak."

"We thank you, sire," Selwyn told the man. "We are grateful for your help."

The woodcutter bowed to each of them in turn. "I am thankful that I can be of service." With these words, he hurried away.

Following the helpful woodcutter's directions, Selwyn, Gilda, and Josiah took the trail to the left. The path was wide and easy to follow, but meandered back and forth repeatedly as it descended a rocky hillside with dense stands of young trees. As the travelers followed the winding trail, they soon found themselves passing through a strange, gray mist that hung just above the ground, obscuring the path.

"It's hard to see the trail," Gilda complained, looking at the unusual mists that swirled around her ankles. "What is this stuff?"

"It's just fog," Josiah answered, swinging his stick and breaking the top from a tall weed beside the trail. "I'm sure it won't hurt us."

The three travelers had no way of knowing it, but they had just entered the Valley of Indifference, a region of hidden swamps and marshes. The harmless-looking mists around their feet were in reality poisonous vapors from the marshes and were known as the Miasma of Lethargy. Had Prince Josiah, Prince Selwyn, and Princess Gilda known how harmful the misty vapors had been to many of the King's messengers before them, they would have fled in haste.

Chapter Six

As Prince Josiah and his companions descended into the Valley of Indifference, they found themselves completely engulfed by the swirling mists. The vapors had now become so thick that the trail was all but invisible, and they had to stay close just to be able to see each other. Unaware of the extreme danger they were in, they pressed on, unconcerned.

"The fog is so thick that I can hardly see," Princess Gilda complained, coughing a bit as a result of the vapors. "How will we know which way to go?"

"Just stay on the trail," Josiah called, bending low in an effort to make out the path through the swirling mists. "The fog can't last forever. If we press on I'm sure we'll soon be out of it." Pausing in the middle of the trail, his body was wracked with a fit of coughing but he failed to notice that anything was amiss.

Prince Selwyn bumped into him. "It's getting harder and harder to see, Josiah. Maybe we should go back and wait until the fog lifts. If we come to a cliff or a drop-off, we could step right off the edge without even knowing that it's there."

Josiah laughed at him. "Your imagination is getting the best of you again, my friend. We're on the trail. Do you think that the trail would lead over the edge of a cliff?" He hurried on. Gilda and Selwyn, not knowing what else to do, followed close behind.

A moment later Josiah spotted a plot of marshy ground bordering the trail. Bending low to examine the spot more closely, the young prince pointed it out to Selwyn. "Look," he said, tauntingly, "we're at the edge of a swamp. Do you think now that we're in danger of falling off the side of the mountain? We're down in a valley. I told you that we're not in danger."

Gilda moved closer. "Listen," she said softly. "What is that sound?"

Selwyn and Josiah both heard it at the same time. From somewhere out in the mists, sounding faint and indistinct as if it were far away, came the soft sounds of a human voice. Somewhere, a young woman was singing. Mysterious, haunting, and incredibly beautiful, the melodic song rose and fell as the sound wafted across the valley. The woman's voice was enchanting, and Josiah felt strangely drawn to the mysterious singer, although he could not see her. He longed to hear more.

"Perhaps we should keep going," Gilda said quietly. Her voice trembled.

"Wait," Josiah replied curtly. "I want to listen. I can't make out the words of the song."

"But I don't like this fog," the girl protested. "It makes me feel uneasy and... afraid."

Josiah had already stepped from the path and was standing at the edge of the miry swamp. "Did you ever hear anything so beautiful?" he said softly to Selwyn, who had appeared through the mists to stand beside him. "Who is she?"

"I don't know." Selwyn's eyes were glazed and held a faraway look, but Josiah didn't notice.

Gilda appeared beside them and took her brother's hand. "I don't like this, Selwyn," she said quietly. "I feel afraid. We need to keep traveling. We must find Everyman and deliver the pardon."

"We'll only be here a moment or two," Josiah said sharply.

"But what about Everyman?" the girl whispered, as if she were afraid to speak aloud. "What if we don't reach him in time?"

"If we don't find him in time, someone else will. We're not the only servants King Emmanuel has, you know."

Intimidated by Josiah's gruff manner, Gilda nodded and fell silent.

The mysterious song continued, soft and melodious and enchanting. The melody was at the same time both lonely and mournful, creating a deep sense of emptiness within the soul of the listener, and yet at the same time it was exhilarating and stimulating, creating the desire to hear more. Selwyn and Josiah, enchanted by the voice of the unknown singer, stepped from the trail and began to make their way through the swamp. Their boots sank deeply into the mire, but, completely mesmerized as they were by the haunting melody, neither youth noticed.

"Selwyn, wait!" Gilda called. "Josiah, wait! Come back! We must stay on the trail and continue with our search for Everyman."

The two young princes ignored her and plodded on through the muck and mire. Terrified at the thought of being left behind in the swirling mists, the frightened girl stepped reluctantly from the trail and hurried after them. The mud of the swamp rose around her ankles, pulling at her feet with an unrelenting suction that frightened her, but she plunged on ahead resolutely.

Josiah also noticed the curious suction that pulled at his boots. It was as if the swamp was determined to swallow him up, and the sensation was a bit frightening. Ignoring his fears, the young prince slogged through the slimy mire. The voice was calling, wooing him, and beckoning him. The muck rose above the tops of his boots, but he failed to notice. His right foot plunged into a void and he fell face forward in the swamp. Struggling to regain his footing, he rose to his feet, covered from head to toe with the foul-smelling slime of the swamp.

He paused. Silence reigned over the marsh—the voice was gone. He stood quietly, head cocked to one side, listening intently. He scanned the marsh, eager for a glimpse of the stranger who sang so alluringly, but all he could see was the swirling mists around him. Selwyn appeared at his elbow. "She stopped," he said quietly, with disappointment written across his face. "She stopped singing. How will we ever find her if she doesn't sing?"

Prince Josiah held up one hand. "Listen."

The enchanting song came again, sounding so tantalizingly near, and yet so far away. Josiah turned. "It's coming from over there now." He started toward the sound. The muck and mire of the swamp was deeper now, but he failed to notice.

"Josiah, wait! Selwyn, wait!" The boys turned. Gilda struggled toward them, lifting each foot high as she fought the unrelenting swamp. The filthy water was higher than her knees. Her gown, hands and arms were caked with mud; her hair was matted, and tiny rivulets of dirty water ran down her face. "Let's go back!" she wailed. "The swamp is getting deeper, and we will soon lose our way. We must find Everyman! If we don't find him—" The alluring voice of the unseen woman grew louder at that moment. Gilda paused in mid-sentence, turned toward the sound, and started in that direction.

Josiah, Selwyn, and Gilda pursued the elusive sound for the next hour. Enchanted by the beauty of the melody, they stumbled blindly through the swamp, always in hopes of catching a glimpse of the mysterious singer. The plight of Everyman was soon forgotten. Mesmerized by the ethereal music and overcome by the poisonous vapors, they had lost sight of their mission for King Emmanuel, lost their concern for Everyman, and forgotten their reason for even coming to the Land of Unbelief. The Valley of Indifference had taken its toll.

Selwyn stopped suddenly and Josiah bumped into him. "Why did you stop?" he demanded irritably. "Keep going! We'll never find her if you keep stopping!"

"Listen," Selwyn replied.

"Listen to what? I don't hear anything."

"That's just it," Selwyn replied. "She stopped singing. I haven't heard her for the last several moments."

"Well, we can't find her if she doesn't sing."

"Keep searching for her," Gilda begged softly.

Josiah ignored her. "Sing," he urged in a whisper, unaware that he was even speaking aloud. "We can't find you unless you sing! Please, sing." But the mystery voice was silent.

The three royal messengers stood quietly in the Swamp of Indifference, listening intently, but the enchanting voice of the mysterious singer was not heard again. They waited and waited, but the lovely melody had died away like an echo in a canyon. The woman had vanished. Deep within his soul, Josiah felt an overwhelming sense of loss.

"Well," Selwyn said with a sigh, "what do we do now?"

Josiah shrugged. "We need to find our way out of this wretched swamp," he replied. "Somehow we need to find our way back to the ship." Already King Emmanuel's mission had been forgotten.

"But which way do we go?" Gilda wailed, staring in dismay at the swirling mists around them. "I have no idea which way we came."

"We came this way," her brother said confidently, turning about and slogging through the mire. After three or four laborious steps he paused and looked about uncertainly. "No, maybe we came from that direction."

Gilda looked up at Josiah. "What do you think?" she asked timidly. "Which way should we go?"

Josiah hesitated. "I—I don't know," he said finally. "I have no idea which direction is which. The fog keeps us from seeing anything very clearly." Selwyn and Gilda watched Josiah expectantly, waiting for him to make a decision. "I think we need to simply walk in a straight line," the young prince said finally. "I have no idea which way we came, but if we just start walking we can get out of this swamp, as long as we don't wander." The others agreed and so they started off, doing their best to keep a straight course through the swirling mists.

An hour later they paused for a brief rest. Josiah noticed a troubled look pass across Selwyn's face. "What's wrong?" he asked.

"That bush with the log lying across it," his friend replied, pointing. "I saw it less than half an hour ago. We've been walking in circles!"

"That's what I was afraid of," Josiah said with a sigh. "But how are we to find our way out of here, if we can't see more than five feet in front of us?"

"The book!" Gilda exclaimed. "Use the book. It will guide you."

Josiah felt a sense of relief as he reached within his doublet for the book. Opening the precious volume, he turned it about until the pages began to glow with a bright light. Reassured, he started forward with his companions right behind him. Ten minutes later, the trio once again found themselves on firm ground, having left behind the Valley of Indifference with its poisonous vapors.

The narrow footpath on which they were now traveling led past a small farm. Two men, strong and solidly built, were busily loading hay onto a crude two-wheeled cart. Hitched to the cart, a steel-gray ox waited patiently. The men looked up from their work as the trio approached, and Josiah could tell by their features that they were father and son.

"Strangers in this region, are you not?" the older man called. "And what is your business in the Land of Unbelief?"

"We're on business for His Majesty, King Emmanuel," Josiah answered proudly, once again remembering their mission. "We have a pardon to deliver to a prisoner in the Dungeon of Condemnation. Would you be so kind as to tell us how we might find it, if you know the way?"

To Josiah's surprise, both peasants burst into laughter. "On business for the King, are you?" the younger man snorted, howling with laughter. "Sure you are! And I'm the Crown Prince of Terrestria!" Both men doubled over, leaning on each other for support and laughing until the tears ran down their faces.

Gilda stamped her foot. "We *are* on business for the King!" she declared angrily. "All three of us are part of the Royal Family. I'm Princess Gilda, and this is Prince Selwyn and Prince Josiah."

"Excuse us, Your Highness," the younger peasant said with a sneer. "We humbly beg your pardon. We didn't realize that we were in the presence of royalty!" He bowed, sweeping his yeoman's cap off his head and bending from the waist in a long, exaggerated bow. His father roared with laughter.

Josiah boiled with anger at the mockery. "Princess Gilda tells the truth!" he said hotly. "You *are* in the presence of royalty. All three of us are the children of His Majesty, King Emmanuel, and we are engaged in a mission for His Majesty."

The older peasant stepped close to Josiah and looked him over from head to toe. "Where did you sleep last night, Your Highness," he taunted, "in a pigsty?" A row of even teeth flashed white in the broad, sunburned face as the man grinned derisively. "Your mouth says that you are royalty, lad, but your garments say otherwise."

Selwyn spoke for the first time. "My sister and my friend are telling you the truth," he said hotly. "Mock us if you will, peasant, but you are indeed in the presence of royalty. We are the sons and daughter of King Emmanuel, and we have come to the Land of Unbelief to deliver the King's pardon to a condemned man."

The peasant stepped backward and looked the three of them over with disdain. "I have never met King Emmanuel, but I find it hard to believe that he would send his children dressed in filthy garments such as you wear." He laughed again. "And if you did find this condemned man of whom you speak, he would not receive the pardon from your hands. My young friends, you do not look like children of the King."

Turning back to the oxcart, he used his pitchfork to pick up a huge clump of hay and hurl it onto the cart. "Come, son," he said, "let us detain our royal visitors no longer. We have work to do, and they are on business for the King!" Both men were laughing as they resumed the work of loading the cart.

Josiah, Selwyn, and Gilda hurried down the trail. "They didn't believe us," Gilda pouted. "We *are* the children of King Emmanuel and we *are* on a mission for our Father, but they didn't believe us."

Josiah was thoughtful. "The peasant was right, though. We *don't* look like the children of King Emmanuel. We weren't careful to keep our garments clean, and now we don't look like the representatives of King Emmanuel at all. I suppose if we were to find Everyman just now and attempt to deliver the pardon, perhaps he would not even listen to us. We didn't keep our garments clean."

Gilda and Selwyn stopped in the middle of the trail. Their faces fell as they examined their hands, arms and clothing, seemingly noticing for the first time that they were caked with mud and slime. "What do we need to do, Josiah?" Selwyn asked quietly. "We can't go looking like this, since we represent King Emmanuel."

Josiah's heart leaped as his gaze fell upon a quiet stream flowing parallel to the path. "The Stream of Forgiveness!" he cried. "I did not expect to see it here in the Land of Unbelief, but it flows from the hill where King Emmanuel died for us, and it will cleanse our garments." Without hesitation Josiah stepped into the water, wading out until the water was so deep that it flowed around his shoulders. "Come on in," he called to Selwyn and Gilda. "This is the cleansing that we so desperately need. Once our garments are clean and spotless, we will be ready to deliver the King's pardon to Everyman."

At Josiah's urging, the brother and sister joined him in the water. Moments later as they stepped from the stream, Gilda gave a shout of joy. "Look at my robe!" she cried in delight. "It's so clean and white that it almost hurts my eyes to look at it."

"My armor shines like the noonday sun," Selwyn said happily.

"And now we are ready to deliver the pardon," Josiah replied, "for we now look like children of the King."

"What happened to us?" Selwyn asked. "How did we allow ourselves to become so covered with that foul mud and slime? It was as if we simply didn't care."

Josiah thought it over. "Sir Wisdom warned us about a place known as the Valley of Indifference," he said slowly. "He said that the poisonous vapors could overcome us so that we would no longer care about fulfilling the King's mission or delivering the pardon to Everyman. Apparently the fog we saw was more than just fog—it was the poisonous vapors that Sir Wisdom warned us of."

"That man was sent by Argamor!" Gilda blurted suddenly. "He was sent to keep us from finding Everyman and delivering the King's pardon."

"What man?" her brother asked.

"The woodcutter who sent us through the valley," the girl answered. "He gave us wrong directions to keep us from reaching the Dungeon of Condemnation and delivering the pardon to Everyman! He was sent by Argamor."

"Aye, you may be right," Josiah told her.

"Then the woman who sang so beautifully was also an agent for Argamor," Selwyn surmised. "She lured us deeper into the Swamp of Indifference for the very same reason—to keep us from reaching Everyman. We lost sight of our mission and almost failed our King."

"Aye, and we soiled our garments," Gilda reminded him. "We might have dishonored the name of King Emmanuel if we had attempted to deliver the pardon when we were in that condition."

"We must be very careful from now on," Josiah told them both. "We must be on the lookout for any more agents of Argamor who will try to stop us from reaching the Dungeon of Condemnation. We must also be careful to keep our garments clean that we might honor the name of His Majesty and that we might deliver the pardon when we find Everyman."

Prince Selwyn and Princess Gilda nodded in agreement.

"We will stop for no one," Prince Josiah declared. "No one will keep us from finding the Dungeon of Condemnation and delivering the pardon to Everyman. Agreed?"

"Agreed," Selwyn and Gilda chorused.

"No matter what happens or who tries to hinder us, we will not stop until we have completed our mission for the King. Agreed?"

"Agreed."

The trio found themselves passing through a forest. The narrow path on which they walked was shaded by tall stands of sturdy oaks, maples and poplar. Occasional rays of golden sunlight penetrated the leafy canopy overhead to form bright pools of light on the dark floor of the forest. Wildflowers grew in abundance on both sides of the trail, creating brilliant splashes of color against the dark green of the forest. White sulfur butterflies danced in the air above the flowers.

"This is a pretty place," Gilda remarked, pausing in the middle of the trail to look about in wonder. "Let's stop and rest awhile."

"We must press on," Josiah told her, "for we lost so much precious time wandering in the Swamp of Indifference."

"Timber!" an urgent voice shouted in warning. The startled young people looked up just in time to see a huge tree crashing down upon them.

Chapter Seven

With a loud cracking, snapping sound, the huge tree fell straight toward Prince Josiah and his two companions, slicing like a giant knife through the canopy of smaller trees around it. Josiah tensed, preparing to leap clear of the danger, but saw that Selwyn and Gilda stood rooted to the spot. Open-mouthed, they stared up at the immense tree about to crush them to the earth.

"Run!" Josiah shouted, leaping forward and shoving his companions with all his might. The tree crashed to the earth behind them with an impact that shook the forest.

Josiah stood shakily to his feet. "Are you all right?" he asked Gilda and Selwyn, who were picking themselves up from the forest floor.

"I—I think so," Gilda replied, brushing bits of grass and leaves from her clothing.

"Josiah," Selwyn said quietly, "that tree would have flattened us had you not pushed us out of the way."

"A thousand pardons, my lords!" A thin-faced peasant hurried forward, clutching a double-bit axe. "Are you all right? The tree was already falling, and then I saw you on the trail, and..." His voice trailed off. A worried look creased his face, and he bit his lower lip nervously. "I ask your pardon, my lords and my lady," he said again. "It was an accident, I assure you! The tree was falling, and I could not stop it, and..."

"Aye, we're all right," Josiah assured him. "The tree came close, but it did not harm us."

A look of relief swept across the woodcutter's face. Dropping his axe, he clasped his hands in front of his face. "I am so thankful," he said softly. "If the tree had injured you..."

A loud groan of distress interrupted his words. Josiah turned in the direction of the sound and gasped in horror. "There is a man beneath the tree!" he cried in dismay. "The tree has pinned him to the earth!"

The woodcutter leaped forward with a look of anguish upon his features. "It is my partner, Diversion," he cried. "He tried to save you, and behold—the tree has fallen upon him!"

The woodcutter gazed at the young people with a beseeching look on his thin features. "You must help me," he begged. "Help me get the tree off my friend. Please, we cannot leave him here to die!"

"We will help you, sire," Josiah promised. "Show us what to do."

The man beneath the fallen tree groaned again.

"Take my axe," the woodcutter urged, pressing the tool into Selwyn's hands. "Fell a small tree to wedge beneath the fallen one. Your friend and I will use the saw to cut my friend free."

Prince Selwyn began to swing the axe against the base of a nearby tree. The woodcutter hurried away, and then reappeared moments later with a long, two-man saw. Prince Josiah manned one end of the big saw and helped cut the fallen tree into sections in order to free the pinned man. Princess Gilda helped by moving branches out of the way. In just minutes they were able to raise a section of the log high enough to drag the injured man from beneath it.

The thin-faced woodcutter knelt beside his friend, whose eyes were closed. "Diversion, are you all right? Speak to me!"

Diversion slowly opened his eyes. "It's my legs," he groaned. "I can't move my legs."

Just then two men appeared on the trail. Spotting the injured man lying on the ground, they immediately rushed over. "What happened?"

"A tree fell on him," the thin woodcutter told them. "He can't move his legs."

"We'll take him back to his hut," the newcomers offered. Carefully lifting the fallen man, they carried him away through the woods.

"We're going to be short a man," the thin-faced woodcutter told the young people. "I need to ask for your help."

"I'm sorry, sire, but we're on a mission for the King and cannot stop to—" Josiah began, but Selwyn cut him off.

"What kind of help do you need from us, sire?"

"A bridge is being built over the stream, and Diversion and I were hauling the lumber for it. Now that he is hurt, we will be short a man and the builders of the bridge will be delayed. You must help us."

"We wish that we could help, sire, but the King's business requires haste," Josiah began again. "Perhaps there are others—"

"What can we do?" Selwyn asked the man.

"We need you to haul timber," replied the woodcutter. "I'll show you what to do."

Josiah stepped close to Selwyn. "We agreed not to stop for any reason, remember?" he said in a low voice. "We must continue until we have found Everyman and delivered the pardon."

"Aye, but this is an emergency," Selwyn argued. "And in a

way, I suppose that we are responsible. The man was trying to save us when he was hurt."

"But we are on the King's business," Josiah insisted. "We must not turn aside! Everyman will perish if the pardon is delayed."

Gilda spoke up. "Selwyn's right," she declared. "We need to stop and help, especially since we were involved in the mishap."

"But we have to keep going! We are on the King's mission."

"Go on without us if you must," Selwyn retorted, "but my sister and I have chosen to stay and help."

Josiah was frustrated. "You're making a mistake."

"So go on without us."

"You know that I can't do that! If we get separated, we'll never find each other again."

"Then do as you want, but Gilda and I are going to stay and help."

The thin-faced woodcutter was watching them closely. Josiah stared at him. "Where have I seen you before, sire?"

"I do not know that you have ever seen me before, my lord. Have you ever traveled through this region before today?"

"Never, sire."

"Then you have never laid eyes on me before this, my lord, for I have lived all of my days in the Land of Unbelief."

"But you look familiar. I know that I have seen you somewhere."

The woodcutter shrugged. "Not unless you have journeyed through the Land of Unbelief, my lord." He turned to Selwyn and Gilda. "My partner and I have cut a number of crossbeams for the bridge, and I can use your help in carrying them to the building site. Follow me, and I will show you where they are."

Selwyn and Gilda followed him readily. Josiah watched them for a moment, shrugged, and then followed along.

66

The woodcutter led them to a stack of freshly cut lumber. "Grab a beam and follow me," he said. "I'll show you where the bridge is being built." Josiah, Selwyn, and Gilda obligingly each shouldered a beam and followed him down the narrow path through the woods. Moments later they came to the site of the bridge.

The structure, half-completed, spanned a narrow, slow-moving river. A sturdy stone abutment on each bank supported the ends of the wooden bridge while the center rested upon a stone pier standing in the middle of the river. Half a dozen workmen were busily putting the finishing touches on the stonework while another crew was adding crossbeams to the supporting framework. A third group of workmen was already preparing to put the planking in place. The building site swarmed with activity.

A stonemason looked up as they approached. "Aye, will you look at that! Unless my eyes deceive me, we now have royalty working for us."

"Place your beams on that pile yonder," the woodcutter told them, ignoring the stonemason. "You know where to find the rest of the beams. I'll get back to work cutting timber."

The three young people spent the next three hours hauling timbers, stone, and mortar for the building of the bridge. On one trip, Josiah noted that the new structure was wide enough for two farm wagons to pass each other easily, but that there was no road leading to the bridge. A narrow footpath meandered down to the bridge approach, and on the opposite side of the river, the riverbank terminated in a sheer granite cliff. The bridge went nowhere.

That's strange, he told himself. *Why would they build a bridge that leads to a dead end? This bridge is useless!*

The thin-faced woodcutter came down to the bridge just then to check on their progress and noticed that Josiah was study-

THE SEARCH FOR EVERYMAN

ing the bridge. "Back to work, my young friend," he prompted. "There is much to be done. One must never stand idle."

"Distraction," one of the workmen called to the woodcutter, "give the lad a chance to catch his breath. There's no need to work him until he drops."

"We have our orders," the woodcutter retorted sharply. "The bridge must be completed on schedule."

Distraction! The woodcutter is called by the name Distraction! Josiah inhaled sharply. Suddenly he knew where he had seen the thin-faced man before.

He turned and hurried back into the woods and met Selwyn coming down the trail with a heavy beam on his shoulder. "I know where I've seen the woodcutter before," Josiah said urgently. "He is called by the name Distraction. He works for Argamor!"

Selwyn stared at him. "Are you certain?"

"Aye," the young prince replied. "I was on a mission for King Emmanuel one day when Distraction stopped me and asked me to help him catch a chicken. I caught the chicken instead of attending to the King's business, and, as a result, failed in my mission. Later I realized that Distraction had been sent by Argamor to keep me from doing the King's business."

Selwyn looked skeptical.

"Selwyn, that's exactly what's happening today! We're busy on a worthless project instead of carrying out the King's mission. Distraction is keeping us from delivering the pardon to Everyman."

"I'd hardly say that building a bridge is a worthless project, Josiah. And we do have a certain obligation here, you know. Diversion was injured while trying to keep us from getting hurt by the falling tree. We're just taking his place."

"I think that whole thing was staged," Josiah told him.

"Remember what we were talking about just before the tree fell? We had just agreed that we would let nothing stop us from reaching Everyman with the pardon. Moments later the tree falls and here we are, delayed again."

"Are you saying that you think Diversion was not really hurt?"

Josiah nodded. "I think the entire episode was just a charade to distract us from the King's business."

Selwyn shook his head. "Josiah, that's preposterous! And I think you'll have to agree that we have an obligation to help since Diversion was hurt trying to save us."

Josiah sighed. "Then look at the bridge we're building, Selwyn. It leads nowhere! Did you see the riverbank on the other side? There's a cliff there that must be at least eighty feet high. There's no place to build a road. Why are we building a bridge in such a place?"

Selwyn frowned. "There's a cliff there?"

"Just beyond the bridge. Didn't you see it? The bridge goes nowhere!"

"I guess I was too busy working to notice," Selwyn admitted.

"We need to leave this place immediately and resume our journey to the Dungeon of Condemnation," Josiah insisted. He glanced upward. "There's barely an hour of daylight left. Let's find Gilda and tell her that we're leaving immediately."

"I heard my name," Gilda's voice announced, as she stepped around a bend in the trail. She was carrying a sack full of wooden pegs for the bridge. "Why aren't you two working?"

"Gilda, we need to leave here immediately," Josiah told her.

A puzzled frown appeared on her pretty face. "Why?"

"Josiah says that the woodcutter is an agent for Argamor," Selwyn offered, and the tone of his voice told Josiah that his friend still did not fully believe him.

"His name is Distraction, and he works for Argamor," the young prince explained. "Once, when I was on a mission for King Emmanuel, he distracted me from the King's business and got me doing something else."

"Chasing a chicken," Selwyn snorted.

"A chicken?" Gilda looked confused.

"There's no time to explain now," Josiah said hastily. "Anyway, Distraction kept me from the King's business and as a result I failed in my mission for His Majesty. Gilda, that's what he's doing to us today! We're building this useless bridge instead of taking King Emmanuel's pardon to Everyman."

"But we have to help," the girl replied. "Diversion was hurt because of us. We're just taking his place."

"That's what Distraction wants us to think," Josiah told her. "But I think that the whole episode with the falling tree was a charade to draw us away from our mission."

Gilda was thoughtful. "What should we do?"

"We need to leave right now," Josiah insisted. "Drop the lumber pegs and let's hurry away from here as fast as we can go."

"back to work!" an angry voice snarled. "You three aren't anywhere until the bridge is finished!"

Josiah and his companions turned to see Distraction in the middle of the trail with an angry expression on countenance. In his right hand he held a glittering him stood six workmen with drawn swords.

"behind us," Josiah said quietly, as the men toward them. The slender princess sought refuge of an outcropping of granite. The boys took front of her. Josiah turned to Selwyn. "These and they are determined to stop us at any ght for King Emmanuel."

Chapter Eight

Prince Josiah's heart raced as the seven armed men stalked toward him and Prince Selwyn. He reached within his doublet and felt a calm assurance when his fingers closed around the book. "Draw your sword," he said softly to his companion, "and remember that we fight in the strength of King Emmanuel!"

There came a terrific crashing sound from the bushes beside the trail, and the two young princes turned to see five more armed men step into view. Josiah was not surprised to see that Diversion was among them. Both boys drew their swords, and at the same instant, their opponents were suddenly clad in dark armor.

"It's twelve against two," Selwyn quavered, looking about in terror as the two groups of dark knights advanced upon them. "We don't stand a chance!"

"We fight in the name of King Emmanuel," Josiah answered quietly, "with swords that were fashioned by the King himself. We have the Shield of Faith. The victory is ours, Selwyn, for there is no restraint to our King to save by many or by few. And don't forget that Gilda also wields a sword."

"Throw down your swords, lads," Distraction called, "or you will never leave this spot alive!"

"We serve King Emmanuel," Josiah replied evenly. "By whose authority do you seek to detain us?"

"By the authority of Lord Argamor," Distraction answered, "sovereign ruler of the Land of Unbelief and Lord of all Terrestria!"

"There's your proof, Selwyn," Josiah whispered to his companion. "King Emmanuel is Lord of Terrestria," the young prince cried, "and Argamor is merely a usurper who would attempt to seize His Majesty's throne!"

"Hold your tongue, lad!" Distraction shouted. "Drop your sword— or prepare to die!"

Josiah glanced at Selwyn and saw that his face was white and that his sword was trembling. "Trust in your King," Josiah whispered.

"Th-there are t-twelve of them," Selwyn stammered.

"And they are doomed to defeat," Josiah replied. Raising his sword aloft, he shouted with all his might, "We fight in the name of His Majesty, King Emmanuel, and for the honor of his name!"

Both groups of dark knights came charging in at that instant, and the battle was joined. Gripping his invincible sword with both hands, Prince Josiah swung the mighty weapon with all his strength. The gleaming blade cut cleanly through the armor of the nearest dark knight, inflicting a mortal wound. The man retreated quickly.

A second knight came dashing in, swinging his sword furiously, and steel clashed against steel as Josiah met the assault. Josiah fought furiously, meeting each thrust of the enemy's sword with a parry of his own blade. Within moments, the second knight was seriously wounded and retreated hastily.

Josiah glanced over at Selwyn and saw to his relief that his friend was beating back the advances of two dark knights.

Screaming furiously, the entire band of enemy knights charged in. Prince Josiah and Prince Selwyn stood shoulder to shoulder, meeting each blow of the enemy swords with the Shield of Faith and the Sword of the Spirit. The clearing rang with the sounds of the conflict—the clash of sword against sword, the shouts and cries of the combatants, the dull clank of swords striking shields and armor. Argamor's band of dark knights could not stand before the invincible power of the mighty swords wielded by the two young princes. Shouting the name of their King and swinging their swords with all their might, Selwyn and Josiah drove the enemy backwards.

"We have them on the run, Josiah!" Selwyn exulted, his eyes wide with astonishment. "There are a dozen of them, but they cannot stand before us!"

"I wish Sir Faithful could see me now," Josiah replied, thrusting with his sword and dealing an enemy knight a mortal blow. "I don't think he realizes how well he taught me, or how well I can wield a sword."

Selwyn laughed. His face was flushed with excitement, and he was clearly enjoying the sweet taste of victory. "May I remind you that you're not the only one engaged in this battle against evil? I'd say that my sword is also doing rather well. Distraction didn't know what he was getting into when he challenged the two of us, did he?"

At that moment the tide of the battle turned, and the two young princes suddenly found themselves driven backwards by an unexpected assault. Within moments they had lost every bit of ground that they had gained and found themselves forced back against the rocky ledge where Gilda stood.

"What happened, Josiah?" Selwyn cried in dismay. "We were easily winning the victory over these evil ones, and now they are about to overcome us!"

An enemy knight swung a vicious blow just then, and Josiah failed to get his Shield of Faith up in time. The sword pierced Josiah's armor, inflicting a serious wound to his shoulder. Josiah reeled in pain. Anxious to follow through, the knight lifted his sword for a second blow. Selwyn came to Josiah's rescue, leaping in and desperately swinging his sword as he drove the knight back. Gilda swung her sword with both hands, inflicting a mortal wound to the enemy knight. With a crash of armor, he fell to the ground.

"Selwyn! Beware!" Gilda screamed. A tall knight had leaped in between Selwyn and Josiah. Raising his sword with both hands, he clearly intended to take off Selwyn's head. Josiah saw what was about to take place. Unable to raise his sword in time to fend off the blow, he lowered his head and charged straight into the enemy knight, knocking him off balance. With the clatter of armor both combatants tumbled to the ground.

Panting heavily, Selwyn leaped out of the midst of the danger and dashed to the rock. Holding his sword at the ready, he stood with his back to the rock as he attempted to catch his breath. Josiah rolled free, leaped to his feet, and managed to reach Selwyn safely.

"This is it, Josiah," Selwyn panted. "I can't take much more, and you are wounded. We're losing the battle. The enemy knights have won!"

"Oh, no, they haven't," Josiah declared fiercely through gritted teeth. "We are losing because we grew overconfident and started trusting in ourselves and our own abilities. Our pride has been our downfall. We must trust in our King, Selwyn, for only then shall we win the battle. But we are not yet defeated."

Raising his sword high, the young prince cried, "For the honor and glory of King Emmanuel!" His shoulder throbbed with pain but he gritted his teeth and charged forward, swinging the glittering weapon with all his strength. Selwyn was at his side. Shoulder to shoulder, the two young princes valiantly fought their way through the band of dark knights. "Fight in the strength of King Emmanuel," Josiah called to his companion. "We cannot win the battle in our own strength!"

A tall knight leaped forward swinging a heavy mace at Josiah's head. Josiah took the blow with his Shield of Faith, and then put the enemy knight to flight with the Sword of the Spirit.

"His strength becomes our strength as we trust him for it," Selwyn agreed, swinging his sword furiously to meet the attack of two dark knights. "We dare not attempt to fight this battle in our own strength, for then we must surely be defeated." One of the enemy knights leaped forward at that instant, thrusting viciously with his sword as he attempted to run the blade through Selwyn's heart. The young prince met the attack with his Shield of Faith and then used his sword to vanquish the adversary.

"And King Emmanuel must receive the glory when we are victorious," Josiah said, "for in reality, the battle is his." He lifted his sword high. "For the honor of King Emmanuel!"

Shouting the name of their great King, Prince Josiah and Prince Selwyn advanced steadily forward, driving the enemy before them. The clearing rang with the sounds of the conflict. Gilda held her position beside the rock, using her own sword to defend herself as she watched the furious battle.

Josiah raised his shield just in time to protect himself from the violent blow of a sword. His adversary, a tall knight whose shield bore a fiery dragon as his coat of arms, swung his great sword with both hands. Screaming with fury, the enemy knight rained blow after blow down upon the young prince, moving so quickly that Josiah was hard pressed to meet the assault. "Help me, King Emmanuel!" he cried. Meeting the blow of the enemy sword with his shield, Josiah swung his own sword with all his might. The steel blade sliced cleanly through the dark knight's shield, shattering his armor and inflicting a terrible wound. The knight fell to the ground.

A dark knight with sword drawn slipped quietly up behind Selwyn. "Selwyn!" Gilda called. "Beware!" Swinging her own sword with both hands, the girl dashed bravely forward and brought the weapon down hard against the back of the knight's helmet. The man crumpled to the ground.

"Gilda," Josiah teased, "that wasn't ladylike!"

Gilda shrugged in mock despair. "A thousand pardons, my lord. I hope that my actions haven't made a bad impression upon you."

Selwyn laughed as he looked at the badly dented helmet on the motionless form of the knight upon the ground. "Your actions, my lady, made quite a lasting impression upon that unfortunate knight!" He hugged her. "Thanks, Gilda."

Josiah laughed. He took a deep breath and looked around. Several dark forms lay motionless upon the ground, but there were no dark knights ready to do battle. "Where is the enemy?" he called.

Selwyn was breathing heavily. "We have won the battle in the name of King Emmanuel!" he exulted. "The enemy knights who have not been killed or severely wounded have fled for their lives. The victory is ours."

Josiah raised his sword triumphantly. "And the glory belongs to King Emmanuel."

Selwyn lowered his sword as he walked over to Josiah. "How is your shoulder?"

"It hurts badly," Josiah admitted. "You can help me bandage it as soon as we know for certain that the enemy will not return." He smiled ruefully. "Perhaps it will serve as a reminder to me not to trust in my own strength the next time we face an adversary."

Gilda lowered her sword as she eyed the fallen forms upon the ground. "I was so afraid," she whispered. "For a few moments it looked as if those knights were going to kill us all. There were so many of them."

"King Emmanuel gave us strength," her brother replied. "When we remembered to trust in him instead of in ourselves, we won the victory."

Josiah's shoulder was soon bandaged and the royal trio once again set out on their mission. "Nothing will stop us now," Josiah declared. "We must find the Dungeon of Condemnation and deliver the pardon to Everyman."

The path upon which they traveled led down to the edge of a small, winding river, then turned and began to follow its banks. Large willows hung gracefully over the path, providing shade as they walked along. Before long they came to a gristmill. Pausing in the middle of the trail, they watched the waterwheel as it turned round and round, spilling water into a narrow channel.

Princess Gilda laid a gentle hand on Josiah's arm. "Listen," she said softly. "I hear someone weeping."

The boys paused, listening intently. Barely audible above the buzz of insects were the quiet sounds of a woman crying. Josiah looked around.

Gilda pointed. "Over there."

Slumped against the stone wall of the mill, partially hidden from view by the deep green leaves of an elderberry bush, was a peasant woman. Her face was buried in her hands and she sobbed as if her heart would break. Josiah, Gilda, and Selwyn walked timidly forward.

Prince Josiah cleared his throat. "My good woman," he said quietly, completely unsure as to how to begin, "it appears that you are in deep trouble. How can we help?"

The woman did not even raise her head. "Alas, no one can help me," she sobbed. Rocking back and forth in her grief, she let out a wail of anguish. "It is too late."

"But—but we would like to try," Josiah said timidly, swallowing hard and wishing for the right words to say. "Will you please let us try to help?"

"Nay, no one can help me," the woman said again. "It is too late, too late, too late." She let out another wail. "Oh my poor, poor husband!"

Josiah looked at Selwyn and Gilda for help, but they both stood silently, staring first at the woman and then at him. The young prince cleared his throat again. He stepped forward and placed a gentle hand on the woman's shoulder. "What is the problem with your husband?" he asked quietly. "Is there something we can do?"

"There's nothing that anyone can do!" the woman wailed. She lowered her hands and raised her eyes to look at Josiah for the first time. Josiah saw an attractive young woman in her middle twenties. Her dark eyes were filled with misery as she silently studied Josiah's face, then turned and looked at Gilda and Selwyn. Sobs racked her body and she lowered her face into her hands again. "Alas, it is too late for my poor husband," she wailed, again rocking miserably from side to side like a small child. "There's nothing that anyone can do."

"Please tell us what the trouble is," Josiah said softly.

"Alas, what will we do when my poor husband is gone?" the peasant woman moaned, as if she had not heard him. "Whatever will my little child and I do?"

"Tell us how we can help," Gilda said softly.

The woman lowered her hands until her eyes were just visible above the tips of her fingers. "Please, leave me alone. There's nothing that anyone can do now. It's too late."

Josiah gently squeezed her shoulder. "Please, tell us what is wrong," he requested softly.

"My poor husband is in the dungeon, he is," the woman whispered in a voice that was barely audible, "though if the truth be known, I am just as guilty as he."

"Why—why is he in the dungeon?" The question came from Selwyn.

"He runs the mill," was the whispered reply. "Or at least he did, that is, until it was discovered that he was shorting the farmers who came to have their corn and wheat ground. I had a part in it too, I did, but the constable took just him to the dungeon. And now I have learned—" The mournful woman dropped her face into her hands and began to sob again. "My poor husband is to be executed! Alas, they are going to hang him, and there's nothing that I can do!"

Her body shook with convulsive sobs. Josiah, Selwyn and Gilda stood helplessly by, uncertain as to what to do.

The woman raised her head. "We have a two-year-old daughter, we do, and what will my child do without her father? I even went to the constable, I did, and offered to take my poor husband's place, seeing how I was involved in the stealin' too. But the constable wanted no part of it and told me that my husband would hang within a week! And that was three days ago."

Josiah looked at Selwyn and Gilda and then turned back to the woman. "Perhaps we can help. We are the children of King Emmanuel, and perhaps—"

"Nay, there's nothing anyone can do for my poor sweetheart," the woman sobbed. "Now, please, just let me be. Woe is me, that I should see such a day!"

"Please, good woman, by what name is your husband called?" Gilda asked, taking the woman's callused hand in her own small, smooth ones. "Please tell me."

The peasant woman looked up at her. "I see not how it matters to you, my lady, but his name is Everyman. Nathaniel Everyman."

The young princess gave a little shriek of joy. She turned to Josiah. "Tell her, Josiah! Tell her!"

Josiah was puzzled by the girl's reaction. "Tell her what, Gilda?"

Gilda was jumping up and down. "Pray tell her about King Emmanuel's pardon. Josiah, her husband is called by the name Everyman! We found him! We found Everyman! If she knows where the dungeon is, we can deliver the pardon to Everyman!"

Chapter Nine

Princess Gilda jumped up and down with joy and then hugged the peasant woman. "We have a pardon for your husband!" she exclaimed, dancing about in her delight. "A pardon from His Majesty, King Emmanuel."

The woman looked up hesitantly at the three young people. "It's true, good woman," Selwyn assured her. "King Emmanuel has issued a pardon for your husband. He is now a free man."

The woman bit the back of her knuckles and began to cry again. "If only it were so." She dropped her head and her sobs shook her entire body. "Oh, if only it were so!"

Josiah withdrew his book from his doublet and then produced the pardon. He unrolled the document and showed it to the woman. "Here it is, good woman, signed by the King's own hand and sealed with his royal seal. Your husband is now a free man! He has been pardoned by His Majesty, King Emmanuel. This document makes it official."

Everyman's wife raised a trembling hand to her mouth. The look of despair upon her face was slowly replaced by one of hope. "How can this be true?" she asked softly, not quite ready to believe the message that she was hearing from the lips of her three visitors. "Is it really true? Can such a thing be?"

"Aye, it's true, good woman," Josiah assured her, holding the precious parchment open for her inspection. "See for yourself! This is the pardon for your husband, and it was issued by King Emmanuel himself."

The miller's wife glanced at the parchment, and then back at Josiah's face. "I cannot read, my lord, but if you say it is true, then it must be true." A look of elation spread across her face as she stood to her feet. "Let's go to him right now, shall we?" She clasped her hands in delight. "They won't hang him! Oh, I can't wait to see the look upon his face when I tell him that he is a free man!"

Impulsively, she hugged each of them. "Thank you for bringing me this piece of wonderful news," she told them, with tears of joy streaming down her face. "This is the happiest day of my life!" Dipping her hands in the water at her feet, she washed the tears from her eyes. "Let me fetch my little one and then we'll be off."

The miller's wife ran to the door of a small cottage hidden among the trees, disappeared inside, and then reappeared almost immediately. She was clutching a small, curly-haired child who was sleepily rubbing her eyes with the back of her fists. "This is Matilda," the happy mother told them. "I woke her up from her nap, but I know that she will be delighted to see her father."

She looked from one visitor to another. "Are we ready?"

Prince Josiah nodded. "Lead the way, good woman."

The trek to the Dungeon of Condemnation where Everyman was being held took almost two hours. Josiah, Gilda, and Selwyn took turns carrying Matilda. Everyman's wife bubbled over with joy. "Oh, you don't know how happy I am," she said repeatedly. "Thank you, thank you for bringing the wonderful pardon for my husband. This is the happiest day of my life!"

Josiah felt a warm glow inside. "We are honored that King Emmanuel chose us to deliver it," he said quietly.

The sun was hanging low in the sky as the little party made their way over the crest of a rocky hill. "There it is!" Everyman's wife exclaimed, pointing. "We're almost there."

A huge, ominous structure of dark stone lay in the fog-shrouded valley below. The setting sun cast its dying rays across the massive walls, sturdy gates and tall towers, giving them a reddish hue. Josiah knew that the forbidding building was the Dungeon of Condemnation, and he shuddered as he looked at it.

"There's no time to lose," Selwyn urged. "Darkness is almost upon us, and they'll soon be locking the gates for the night." Together, they hurried down the path and approached the gloomy dungeon. The walls towered above them, imposing and ominous.

A guard challenged them at the main gate. "What is your business here?" he growled.

"We—we have come with a pardon for one of y-your prisoners," Josiah managed to croak, surprised to realize that he was trembling. *What's wrong with me?* he asked himself. *I'm a child of the King! Why should this man, a mere servant of Argamor, frighten me?*

"Be off with you!" the guard snapped. "We have no time for such foolishness!"

"You must open to us," Josiah demanded. "We have a pardon for one of the prisoners."

"I know of no such pardon," the guard snarled. "Now, be off with you!" Tipping back his head, he called to his companions high atop the wall, "Bar the gate!"

Josiah stepped closer. "But you must open to us," he insisted. "We have a pardon for Everyman."

Selwyn joined him. "The pardon is from His Majesty, the

King. You must open the gate at once and allow us to deliver it to Everyman."

The guard drew his sword. His dark eyes glittered with hatred. "I'll give you a count of five," he threatened, advancing slowly toward them, "and then I take off your heads!"

Everyman's wife whimpered and took a step backwards, and the surly guard glanced in her direction. "The women, too," he growled. "Be off with you now, or I take off all your heads!"

Selwyn and Josiah drew their swords at the same instant. "We come in the name of King Emmanuel," Josiah insisted, "and you *will* open to us!"

"I gave you fair warning, and now it will be a pleasure to take off your heads," the guard said, grinning with anticipation as he stalked toward them. With a snarl of rage, he was suddenly upon them, furiously swinging his sword.

Josiah met the attack with the steel of his own blade. After a few seconds of vigorous fighting, he dealt the guard a deadly blow, and the man fell to the pavement at his feet. The young prince strode forward. When he touched the latch on the massive iron gate, the barrier slowly swung open by itself. "Come on," he urged the others, "let's hurry!"

Four well-armed soldiers met them in the entryway below the gatehouse. "What is your business here?" they challenged.

"We come in the name of King Emmanuel," Josiah replied boldly, displaying the parchment with one hand but holding his sword ready in the other. "We have a pardon from His Majesty for one of your prisoners, a man by the name of Everyman."

One of the guards stepped forward, snatched the parchment from Josiah's hand, and scanned it quickly. "Summon Captain Exclusion," he called to his companions. One of the guards quickly disappeared down a shadowy corridor of the dungeon.

A huge, mean-tempered officer strode angrily into the light. "What is the meaning of this?" he barked. "Who is causing all the trouble?" His gaze fell upon the group standing timidly in the entryway, and he strode over. "Who are you?" he challenged. "What is your business here?"

"Sire, we have a pardon for one of the prisoners," Josiah began, "and we are to have him released—"

"None of our prisoners will ever be released!" the huge man bellowed. "They are all under the sentence of death, and that sentence will be carried out." He gestured toward the gate. "Now, be gone."

Josiah stood his ground. "We have a pardon, sire, from King Emmanuel himself. We demand that the prisoner be released immediately. You have no authority to hold him."

Captain Exclusion drew his sword. "The sentence of death has been passed upon every prisoner in this dungeon, and not a single one of them is to be released," he declared. "I will not repeat myself. Now, you are to leave immediately."

"Not without the prisoner Everyman," Josiah announced flatly.

The captain's features were contorted with rage. "Then I shall chop you into little pieces and feed you to the buzzards," he announced, advancing menacingly toward them with his sword raised.

Josiah quickly unrolled the pardon parchment. "We have been sent by His Majesty, King Emmanuel," he declared. "This pardon for Everyman was issued by King Emmanuel, and therefore you have no authority to hold the prisoner. We demand his release."

Captain Exclusion paused with sword raised as he thought it through. Finally, he lowered the sword in frustration. He turned to one of the guards. "Take these... these people to the prisoner that they seek. Release him and be done with it!"

"Aye, sire," the guard replied quietly. He took a sputtering torch from the wall and turned to the royal visitors. "Follow me."

"Take the wretched prisoner and be gone," the huge captain snarled at Josiah and his companions. "Don't ever set foot within these walls again—or you will regret it, I assure you."

The flickering torch did little to dispel the darkness as the guard led the silent group into the heart of the dismal Dungeon of Condemnation. Grotesque shadows danced on the cold stone walls of the narrow corridor that seemed to wind its way down into the very heart of the earth. The footfalls of the group echoed and reechoed through the dark passageway. Water seeped down the walls to flow across the floor in little rivulets. A large rat dashed past them in the darkness, and Gilda stifled a scream.

Josiah shuddered. His heart pounded as if it wanted out of his chest. The frightful atmosphere in the Dungeon of Condemnation was too much like the dungeon in which he had spent so many nights before King Emmanuel had set him free.

They came to a point where the narrow corridor intersected another, and the guard took the passageway to the left. "This way."

This corridor was lined on both sides with prison cells. The flickering torch illuminated the narrow chambers as they passed, revealing some of the most pitiful wretches that Prince Josiah had ever seen. Empty, lifeless eyes stared back from the darkness. Skeletal hands clutched the bars. Tears welled up in Josiah's eyes. These doomed souls—men, women, and children—were the captives of Argamor, and the sentence of death was upon every one of them. Josiah's heart cried out in anguish at the thought.

A tiny hand reached through the bars as the flickering torch passed one cell, and Josiah saw the pitiful face of a child in the dark recesses of the filthy chamber. "Help me," a pathetic voice called softly, hopelessly. "Won't somebody help me?"

Gilda burst into tears. "Can't we do something?" she begged. "Someone has to do something!" She reached out and touched the child's arm. Tiny fingers grasped her wrist in a grip of desperation.

"Silence," the guard growled, hurrying along the dark corridor. "Move faster!"

Gilda let out a wail as she pulled free from the child's grasp and hurried to keep up with the others. Josiah saw the look of despair that swept across the tiny prisoner's face and he felt as if his own heart were being torn out.

The flickering torch hurried past cells containing prisoners of all ages. Josiah saw men whose faces were filled with despair, women who had given up hope. He saw the empty stares of helpless youth, heard the crying of frightened children. He saw the feeble, twisted bodies of old men and women. And all of them were doomed to die. Sorrow overwhelmed him, settling with such a heavy weight upon his chest that he could scarcely breathe.

He looked at the miller's wife and saw that her face was filled with terror. She clutched her little daughter fearfully to her chest.

An old woman stood with her body pressed against the bars of her cell. As the flickering torch approached, she reached a thin hand toward the little group. Silently, wordlessly, she was clearly asking for help.

"Can't we do something for these poor people?" Gilda cried out again as they passed the desolate woman. Josiah's heart ached.

Moments later the guard paused before a cell and held his torch high. "Everyman? Nathaniel Everyman? On your feet, wretch!"

The miller's wife sprang forward eagerly, but after one glimpse of the cell's occupant her countenance fell. "Guard," she said in a trembling voice filled with disappointment, "this is the wrong cell. That is not my husband."

The prisoner had been sitting upon the cold stone floor with his head down between his knees. As the group approached the bars he raised his head, and Josiah saw a gray, lifeless face with sunken eyes, matted brown hair, and a long beard. The man stood slowly, painfully, to his feet. His tall, battered frame was so thin that he had the appearance of a living skeleton. His hands were white and trembling as they gripped the bars.

"Guard," the miller's wife said again, stepping away from the bars, "you have brought us to the wrong cell. This is the wrong man. This is not my husband."

"Rachel?" the skeleton croaked. "Rachel, is that you?"

The woman gave a cry of anguish. "Nathaniel! Oh, Nathaniel!" Springing forward, she reached through the bars and grabbed the pitiful figure in an embrace with one arm as she held her child with the other. "Oh, Nathaniel, I didn't even know you!"

The tall prisoner was sobbing as he stroked the curly hair of his child with his left hand and the face of his wife with his right. "Rachel, Rachel. My dear, precious Rachel. And my dear little Matilda. I never thought that I would see your lovely faces again."

Josiah swallowed hard. The tears streamed down his face. He looked at Selwyn and Gilda and saw that they were crying as well.

"Stand back, stand back," the guard demanded in a flat,

lifeless tone. With the clank of keys and the screech of rusty hinges, he unlocked the cell door.

The miller's wife handed Matilda to Selwyn and sprang into the tiny cell, wrapping her arms around her husband. The tears flowed freely. "Oh, Nathaniel, Nathaniel."

Everyman held her close for a moment. His eyes were closed but Josiah could see that his lips trembled with emotion. He took a deep, sobbing breath, and then, grasping the shoulders of his wife, held her at arms' length. "Rachel," he said in a husky voice edged with sorrow, "you shouldn't have come. This will only make it worse. Dear Rachel, I am to die tomorrow!"

His wife grasped both of his hands in her smaller ones. Her eyes glittered in the light from the torch as she exclaimed, "That is why we have come, darling. The King has granted you a pardon. You are now a free man! They won't hang you!"

Everyman was speechless. His mouth dropped open and he stared wordlessly at his wife. His lips moved, but no sound came out. Suddenly, his face flushed with color and his eyes sparkled with new life. He turned to the guard. "Is it true, sire? Is it true? Am I to be set free?"

The guard grunted and nodded without replying. His eyes smoldered with resentment.

Everyman gave a whoop of elation. He seized his wife and hugged her repeatedly as the tears of joy streamed down his face. Releasing his wife, he stepped from the cell and snatched his daughter from Selwyn's arms. "Did you hear that, Matilda?" He hugged the tiny child so tightly that Josiah was sure that the life would be squeezed from her. "Papa's coming home again! I'm a free man!"

It was a joyous group that followed the surly guard back to the entrance of the Dungeon of Condemnation. Josiah never even noticed the other prisoners in the surrounding cells; his attention was focused on the happy reunion taking place between Everyman and his family. As they reached the main gate, a resentful guard reached up to unbar the huge iron barrier.

With the screeching protest of rusty hinges, the huge gate swung open. Clutching his little daughter to his heart with one hand and embracing his wife with the other, Everyman stepped through to freedom. "I never thought that I would see this day," he whispered, with tears streaming down his face. "I thought that I would be facing the hangman's gallows tomorrow."

Josiah felt a thrill of satisfaction sweep across his soul. "Thank you, King Emmanuel," he whispered, "for allowing us to be the ones to deliver this poor man's pardon."

Selwyn touched his shoulder. "Josiah," he said quietly, "this is the greatest mission that His Majesty could possibly have sent us on. This was better than storming a castle or conquering a city."

"Wait!" a harsh voice called, and the happy group turned as one to see Captain Exclusion striding angrily toward the gate. "Wait just a minute!"

Everyman's face paled with fear. "Is s-something wrong, sire?"

"Prisoner, by what name are you called?" the huge officer demanded, stepping so close to Everyman that he was breathing in his face.

"Everyman, s-sire," the newly released prisoner stammered, with a desperate glance at his wife. "Nathaniel Everyman."

The captain turned on Josiah. "Let me see this man's pardon," he demanded.

"Certainly, sire," Josiah said calmly. Pulling the book from his doublet, he opened it and produced the precious document. He handed it to Captain Exclusion. "Everything is in order, sire. The pardon was signed and sealed by King Emmanuel himself."

"I'll see for myself," the officer growled, unrolling the parchment and squinting at it in the dying light.

Josiah felt a sense of apprehension as the stern captain examined the document. *There's nothing he can do to stop Everyman from walking out as a free man,* he told himself. *King Emmanuel himself has ordered Everyman's release, and there's nothing the captain can do to stop it.*

"Aha!" Captain Exclusion cried, with a note of satisfaction in his voice. He turned around. "Guards! Guards, return the prisoner to his cell. This man is not going anywhere until tomorrow, and then it's only to walk to the gallows!"

Two burly guards sprang forward and seized Everyman by the arms. The miller's wife stepped toward Captain Exclusion with a look of horror in her eyes. In desperation she clutched his arm. "You can't do this, sire! My husband is now a free man!"

The officer laughed in her face. "Your husband is to be returned to his cell, you wretched woman, but just until tomorrow morning. At that time he will be marched to the executioner's gallows."

Josiah's heart was pounding furiously as he addressed the captain. "Everyman is a free man, sire, and I order you in the King's name to release him. The pardon you hold in your hand is signed and sealed by His Majesty, King Emmanuel, and grants a full pardon to this prisoner."

Captain Exclusion grinned maliciously as he turned to face the young prince. "The pardon I hold in my hand may be from King Emmanuel, but if you'll read it carefully, you'll see that it's for *Adam* Everyman. My prisoner is called by the name *Nathaniel* Everyman, and he dies first thing tomorrow morning! My condolences, young prince, but you tried to free the wrong man."

Chapter Ten

Prince Josiah stared into the dancing flames of the campfire. "I felt so helpless!" he cried aloud. "When Captain Exclusion pointed out that we had the wrong man, I wanted to draw my sword and run him through. I would have done anything to set Everyman free. But when I saw that the pardon was not for that poor miller, I realized that there was nothing that any of us could have done."

He bowed his head. "I suppose that even if we could have attempted a rescue by force, it would have been wrong, even if we had succeeded. Everyman could not be set free without the King's pardon."

Prince Selwyn spoke up. "We did our best, Josiah. That's what matters. We did our best for our King, and for this poor miller. We could do no more."

Josiah's heart ached. "But we failed! Everyman will die to-morrow morning." He bowed his head. "I felt so helpless."

Princess Gilda slipped over and sat beside him on the log in front of the fire. Her face was wet with tears. "J-just think what Everyman's poor wife is feeling right now," she sobbed. "She was so happy! She thought that her husband was going to be released, and now—" Sobs choked off the rest of her words.

"But what right does Captain Exclusion have to hold her and little Matilda in the dungeon?" Selwyn declared angrily. "Even if he executes Everyman, he has no right to hold them."

"Well," Josiah said slowly, "Everyman's wife is guilty, too. She admitted that."

"But what about little Matilda?" Gilda asked. "She's just a little child. She had no part in her parents' scheme to cheat people."

Josiah shook his head sadly. "I don't know. Captain Exclusion seemed to think that she was guilty simply because she was the descendant of two people who were guilty."

"But that's not right!" the young princess declared hotly. "How could she be guilty, just because her parents are guilty?"

Josiah shrugged. "It doesn't seem right to me, but then again, I guess I don't understand royal law."

"What will happen to them?" Selwyn asked anxiously. "Do you think—" He let the sentence go unfinished.

Josiah sighed. "Everyman will face the executioner tomorrow morning," he said sadly. "We all know that. I suspect that his wife will be hung tomorrow as well. As for little Matilda, well, I don't know. I just can't imagine them putting a little child to death, can you?"

Gilda sobbed softly.

Her brother scooted over beside her and squeezed her hand. "What a mess we made of things," he said miserably. "We tried to set a man free, and instead, we helped Argamor's forces capture his family. How could we possibly have done any worse?"

Josiah glanced over at Selwyn and realized that he was weeping.

The somber trio sat silently staring into the fire for several minutes. Each was consumed by sorrow for the poor miller and his family, and each felt a deep sense of personal failure. *Our first mission for King Emmanuel,* Josiah thought dejectedly, *and it ends this way.* The fire snapped and popped, throwing sparks heavenward. The insects of the night hummed and buzzed and chirped, but the three young people around the fire were silent.

Selwyn spoke at last. "So what do we do now?"

Josiah sighed. "Continue our search for Everyman, I suppose. And hope that we're in time. I hate to think of failing a second time and allowing another man to die."

"I want to go back to the ship," Gilda said quietly, staring at the flames and not allowing herself to look at either of her companions.

"Why?" her brother asked.

"I can't bear to go through this again. I know we have to camp here tonight, but I want to start back for the ship first thing in the morning."

"We have to deliver the King's pardon to the right man," Josiah replied. "We can't let another man die."

The young princess shook her head. "I can't do this again, Josiah, I just can't!"

"Josiah's right, Gilda, we do have to deliver the pardon. We were commissioned by the King."

Gilda raised her eyes and looked pleadingly at her brother. "I-I can't Selwyn. I just can't! When I saw the look on Everyman's face—" She burst into tears again. "And his poor wife! And little Matilda! We had given them hope, Selwyn, and then suddenly that hope was snatched away like a bully snatching sweets away from a smaller child. It would have been better if we had never come."

"But what about Adam Everyman?" Josiah argued. "Are we just going to let him die, even though he's been pardoned? And what about King Emmanuel? What will he think of us if we return to the Castle of Faith without delivering his pardon? Gilda, I cannot fail my King."

The young princess was sobbing now. Clasping her arms around her knees, she rocked back and forth. "I want to go back to the ship."

"What's all this talk about going back?" The voice came from the darkness beyond the campfire, startling the three young people nearly out of their wits. Josiah leaped to his feet, drawing his sword as he did. Selwyn followed his lead.

A familiar figure strode into the circle of light from the campfire. Josiah stared in disbelief. "Sir Wisdom!"

The old nobleman stopped at the fire's edge and glared at them sternly. "What's all this talk about going back?" he asked again. "You haven't completed King Emmanuel's assignment, have you?"

Josiah didn't know whether he should hug the old man or hide from him. "We failed, sire," he said sadly. "We failed to deliver the King's pardon to the right man."

"So what happened?" The old man's eyes were still stern, intimidating, accusing.

"We made a mess of things, sire." Selwyn spoke without lifting his head. "We delivered the pardon to the wrong man."

"The wrong man?"

"Aye, the wrong man. Sire, we found another man by the name of Everyman. But he was Nathaniel Everyman, not Adam Everyman. The captain was just about to release him when he discovered the mistake, and now things are worse than ever!"

"So you delivered the King's pardon to the wrong man, did you?"

"Aye, sire." Selwyn was struggling to blink back the tears.

"You three listen to me," Sir Wisdom said quietly, kindly.

"King Emmanuel's pardon was for Everyman. It matters not if it's Adam Everyman or Nathaniel Everyman; the pardon is for Everyman! And that includes every woman, too." He stepped around behind the log on which the three dejected young people were seated and briefly touched each of them on the shoulders. "Go back to the Dungeon of Condemnation tomorrow morning before the sun casts its first rays across the ridges. Deliver the pardon to Everyman and his wife before they are marched to the gallows."

"Will Captain Exclusion hang Everyman's wife, too?" Gilda asked, looking over her shoulder at Sir Wisdom.

The old man nodded. "But the King's pardon is for her, too."

Josiah stood to his feet and faced Sir Wisdom. "But, sire, Captain Exclusion refused to release Everyman. He insisted that we were trying to free the wrong man."

"Captain Exclusion is in the service of Argamor, and he would have you believe that King Emmanuel's pardon is not for everyone. But, my friends, King Emmanuel's pardon is for Everyman! It matters not whether the man's name is Adam or Nathaniel, the King's pardon is for anyone and everyone who will receive it."

"But, sire, what if Captain Exclusion refuses to release Everyman? What are we to do then?"

The old man reached inside his robe and withdrew a book identical to the one that Josiah carried. Opening the volume, he pulled out a parchment. "Here," he said, handing the document to Josiah. "This specifies Nathaniel Everyman by name. Captain Exclusion cannot argue with that!" He took out a similar parchment and handed it to Gilda. "And this one is for Everyman's wife."

"What about little Matilda?" Gilda asked as she took the

document. "Do you have one for her, too?"

"Captain Exclusion knows King Emmanuel's law," the old man replied. "Little Matilda cannot be held in the Dungeon of Condemnation until she is old enough to know right from wrong."

"But don't we need a pardon just for her?" Gilda argued.

The old man regarded her with gentle eyes. "Trust me, my dear. Little Matilda is quite safe."

He walked around to the far side of the fire. "Get some sleep, all three of you. You must be back at the main gate of the Dungeon of Condemnation before sunrise, for the pardons must be delivered before Everyman and his wife are marched to the gallows."

Prince Josiah let out a long sigh of relief. "Thank you, Sir Wisdom."

The eastern sky was just beginning glow with soft hues of pink and purple as Gilda, Josiah, and Selwyn made their way down the hillside toward the forbidding walls of the Dungeon of Condemnation. "We must hurry," Josiah urged. "Sunrise is almost upon us, and Everyman and his wife will be executed at dawn. We must not fail to deliver the pardons in time."

Selwyn scrambled down a shale-covered slope and paused to catch his breath. He glanced toward the dungeon. "Josiah! Look!"

Josiah looked toward the Dungeon of Condemnation. His heart sank. In the dim light of the coming morning he could see that the main gate of the dungeon was open and several guards were leading two prisoners outside. Even though the group was some distance away, Josiah immediately knew the identities of the condemned prisoners. "Hurry!" he urged the others.

The trio rushed frantically down the rugged hillside, leaping over fallen logs, scrambling through bushes and briars, jumping across small ravines and gullies. They had to reach the dungeon before it was too late! Josiah fell headlong on a rocky slope, painfully skinning his hands in the process. Ignoring the pain, he leaped to his feet. He threw a desperate glance toward the valley below. The rising sun was just beginning to peek over the ridges to the east. The guards and their prisoners had paused at the base of a tall wooden structure on the south side of the dungeon. Josiah inhaled sharply. The hanging gallows!

As Josiah, Selwyn, and Gilda reached the valley, the guards were already leading two forlorn figures up the stairs of the gallows. "We're too late!" Gilda wailed.

"Oh, no, we're not!" Josiah cried. Summoning every ounce of strength he possessed, he dashed toward the execution site.

Moments later he reached the gallows. Darting past the guard at the bottom of the stairs, he took the steps two at a time. He reached the platform and stopped in dismay. Two hooded figures stood side by side with their hands tied behind their backs. Thick nooses of knotted hemp rope were already in place around their necks. Captain Exclusion stood nearby with a smirk of satisfaction upon his cruel face. "Executioner," he called to the hangman who stood at the lever operating the trapdoors, "do your duty."

"Wait!" Josiah screamed, leaping forward and throwing his body against the lever so that the hangman could not pull it. "Stop the execution! These people have been pardoned!"

Captain Exclusion stared in astonishment for a moment, and then a dark look of anger swept across his face. Drawing his sword, he stepped toward Josiah. "Stand aside, knave," he snarled. "You will not hinder this execution!"

Josiah drew his own sword with one hand and produced the

pardon for Everyman with the other. "Captain," he said boldly, "I order you in the name of King Emmanuel to release these prisoners. His Majesty has issued pardons for both of them."

The big officer grimaced. "We went through this last night, you fool. Your pardon is for the wrong man. Now, stand aside!"

"Read the pardon," Josiah insisted, thrusting the parchment in the man's face while keeping his foot firmly planted against the trapdoor lever. "This pardon specifically names Nathaniel Everyman."

Selwyn and Gilda came scrambling up on the platform at that moment with swords drawn. "Here is a pardon for Rachel Everyman as well," Gilda called, unrolling the parchment she carried. "Both prisoners are to be set free."

Captain Exclusion snatched the pardons from their hands and quickly scanned them both. Josiah saw a look of frustration cross his features as he read the documents. "Pull the lever," he ordered. "This changes nothing. Both prisoners have been condemned to die, and nothing will stop us from carrying out their sentence."

The executioner stepped toward the lever.

Josiah quickly brought his sword up and pressed the tip of the glittering blade against the man's tunic. "Reach for the lever and I will stop you forever," he challenged. "These prisoners have been freed by King Emmanuel, and no one will harm them."

Selwyn stepped around behind the miller and his wife and began removing the nooses from around their necks. As he pulled off their hoods, their shoulders sagged with relief. Moving quickly, he untied their hands and led them toward the stairs. At the bottom of the stairs, several guards drew their swords and blocked their escape.

"Call off your men, Captain," Josiah ordered. "These prisoners are being released by the express order of His Majesty, King Emmanuel, and no one will hinder us!"

Captain Exclusion gritted his teeth and thrust the parchments at Josiah. "Stand back and allow the prisoners to pass," he ordered in a subdued voice.

The guards stepped back sullenly. Selwyn kept his sword ready as he led the miller and his wife down the stairs of the gallows. Josiah and Gilda quickly followed.

"They still have our little girl," the miller's wife said quietly. "What can we do?"

"Where are they keeping her?" Josiah asked.

"She was with us in the cell," the miller told him. "They left her there when they took us out to the gallows."

"Can you lead me to the cell?" the young prince asked.

Everyman nodded confidently.

"You and Gilda take Rachel to that big oak we passed up on the hillside," Josiah told Selwyn. "Everyman and I will return to the dungeon and get Matilda. We'll meet you at the oak."

Selwyn nodded.

Selwyn and Gilda quickly led Rachel Everyman across the valley. Josiah and Everyman hurried toward the main gate of the dungeon. The young prince watched over his shoulder from time to time but to his relief, Captain Exclusion and his men made no move to follow them.

The guards challenged them at the gate, but Josiah simply claimed the authority of the name of King Emmanuel and gained access to the dungeon. "Lead the way," Josiah told the miller, taking a torch from the wall in the main corridor. Gates and doors opened of their own accord as they hurried along the dark passageways and, within minutes, they had reached the cell where the Everyman family had been imprisoned.

"Papa's here, little Sweetheart," Everyman called to his tiny daughter, who sat sobbing within the cell. "Papa's going to take you home."

The cell door snapped open when Josiah touched it. Everyman sprang eagerly inside, snatched up his daughter, and clutched her to his chest. "It's going to be all right, darling."

Josiah touched the sleeve of the miller's threadbare garment. "Let's meet the others at the oak, sir."

⌘

"We came just in time," Gilda remarked as she, Selwyn, and Josiah climbed the steep slope above the valley. "If we had been just a moment later, Everyman and his wife would have been executed."

"King Emmanuel sent us," Josiah replied. "The honor and the gratitude belong to him, for he is the one who pardoned them. We were merely his messengers."

"I am thankful that His Majesty trusted us with this mission," Selwyn said, "and that we were allowed to have a part in their rescue."

"Look!" Gilda cried, pointing. "Down below!"

Prince Josiah turned. Down in the valley, a regal gold-and-white coach pulled by four powerful horses was speeding toward the distant mountains. An overwhelming sense of gratitude and wellbeing swept over the young prince. "The Coach of Grace," he said quietly. "It came for Everyman and his family."

Prince Selwyn smiled. "We must hurry on," he told his companions. "There is yet another pardon that we must deliver before it is forever too late."

Chapter Eleven

"Delivering the King's pardon was the most thrilling thing that I've ever done in my entire life," Prince Selwyn remarked, as he, Princess Gilda, and Prince Josiah hiked along the narrow trail. "Did you see the look on Everyman's face when I pulled the hood off his head? Did you see the look on his wife's face? In that moment I realized that this entire quest had been worthwhile!"

Josiah nodded soberly. "We were able to serve and honor our King today, and for that I am grateful."

"They would have died," Gilda said with a faraway look in her eyes. "I'm glad we didn't turn back."

Josiah nodded again. "I just hope that we reach Adam Everyman in time. He's facing the hangman's gallows, too, you know. Time is running out."

Selwyn turned to Josiah with a concerned expression on his usually cheerful countenance. "How do we know that we are on the right trail? At this point, we still have no idea where the Dungeon of Condemnation even is. It seems that we've been wandering aimlessly in the Land of Unbelief. Isn't there some way we can find out for sure where the dungeon is and head straight for it? Surely there's someone we can ask."

Josiah stopped and sent a petition to King Emmanuel, asking for guidance in finding the Dungeon of Condemnation in which Adam Everyman was imprisoned. As the parchment disappeared over the horizon, he and his companions resumed their journey.

The trail wound its way around and through a cluster of granite boulders that were as big as houses. At one point, two boulders restricted the trail to a passageway so narrow that it could only accommodate one person at a time. As Josiah squeezed through the narrow opening, he spotted a man sitting under a tree studying a map. "Excuse me, sire," Josiah called, and the stranger looked up with a friendly smile. "Is that a map of the Land of Unbelief?"

"Indeed it is, my lord," the man replied. "My name is Compassionate Witness, but you may call me 'Compassion'. How may I be of help, my lord? Would you care to look at my map? Perhaps I can guide you to some particular location?"

"We are looking for the Dungeon of Condemnation," the young prince replied. "A prisoner named Adam Everyman is being held there, and we have a pardon for him."

"Then you three are on a mission for King Emmanuel," Compassion said. He turned his map so that Josiah, Selwyn, and Gilda could see it easier. "At present you are right here," he explained, placing a finger on the map, "and the Dungeon of Condemnation that you seek is over here." He touched another location.

Josiah leaned closer. "This looks like a river," he said, with some confusion. "Sire, are you saying that the Dungeon of Condemnation is in the middle of a river?"

"Aye, the River of Consequence," Compassion explained. "All the rivers in the Land of Unbelief flow into it: the Rivers of Dishonesty, Greed, Selfishness, Immorality, and many, many others. The inhabitants of the Land of Unbelief often toss the garbage of their sinful lives into these rivers, thinking that the deeds are now but memories and the awful effects have been carried away downstream. But the truth of the matter is this—every man, woman, and child must one day cross the River of Consequence, and when he does, the results of his deeds are waiting for him."

Compassion touched the map again. "This is the Island of Procrastination. As you can see, it is situated right in the middle of the river. On the north end of the island is an impenetrable castle known as the Castle of Resistance. It is one of the strongholds of Argamor himself. The Dungeon of Condemnation is in the bottom of this castle, and it is there that you will find the man you seek."

"This won't be easy," Selwyn declared.

Compassion nodded his head. "Aye, my friend, you are correct. Your mission will not be easy. You will encounter serious opposition at the Castle of Resistance. Argamor's forces will do everything in their power to prevent you from entering the castle."

"What should we expect?" Selwyn asked. "How should we approach the castle?"

"Argamor's men undoubtedly know that you are coming, but they don't know exactly when. I would say that a surprise visit would be the best. The easiest way to gain entrance to the castle would be to catch them off guard."

"How would we do that, sire?"

Compassion shrugged. "That I cannot tell you. Just keep in mind that a surprise visit would be the best—if you can find a way to slip up on the castle and catch the guards unaware, you will gain entrance that much easier. If you have to fight your way in, well..."

Josiah studied the map, trying desperately to memorize the

details. Compassion noticed. "Here, my lord, keep the map," he offered, handing the parchment to the young prince. "It will be of great assistance in your search for Everyman."

The three young people were grateful. "Thank you, sire," they said in unison.

"I am glad that we met you here, Compassion," Gilda told him. "You have been a great help to us already."

"King Emmanuel sent me, of course," the man said with a gentle smile.

Selwyn frowned. "Then why did he not send you sooner?" he wondered aloud. "Truly, sire, we could have used your guidance earlier. We have been wandering around with no real sense of direction or knowledge of where we were going. We have sent petitions, but it seemed that His Majesty was not answering."

"Oh, King Emmanuel's timing is flawless, I assure you," Compassion replied with a chuckle. "He wanted you to find Nathaniel Everyman on your own in order that you might develop a burden for those who are condemned and realize a sense of urgency in delivering pardons to those who will receive them."

"We thank you for your assistance, sire, but we really must be moving along," Josiah said, rolling up the map and stowing it inside his doublet next to the book. "Time is passing rapidly, and we must find Everyman and deliver the King's pardon before it is too late."

Compassion nodded. "Indeed. The King's business requires haste. Farewell, my young friends. I wish you a safe and prosperous mission for our King."

It took another day and a half of difficult travel to reach the River of Consequence. Following the map, Josiah and his two

companions walked for miles and miles across a vast, arid wasteland of skepticism and unbelief. The winds of adversity howled
and shrieked, throwing dust and sand in their faces and doing
their best to discourage them and turn them out of the way, but
the three young people pushed resolutely onward. After a time
they came to a region full of dangerous bogs and treacherous
quicksands, but they refused to be sidetracked. Walking carefully so as not to become mired in the many pitfalls of the area,
they crossed the region safely. On the morning of the second
day they even faced highwaymen who tried to rob them of
their courage, compassion, and dedication, but they fought the
robbers off with their invincible swords and emerged from the
skirmish unscathed and victorious. Finally, late in the afternoon
of the second day, they reached their destination.

"So this is the River of Consequence," Selwyn said, gazing
out across the broad, swift-flowing watercourse before them.
"It looks vile and disgusting."

"Aye, it smells that way, too," Gilda remarked, holding her
nose.

"Compassion told us that all the rivers of the Land of
Unbelief dump their filth into this one," Josiah replied.

The River of Consequence flowed with a powerful current,
surging and pounding its way along, throwing spray high into
the air over the huge boulders that obstructed its path. A foul
smell permeated the air, and an unsightly brownish-yellow
froth hugged the bank of the river, giving evidence of the
poisons that polluted the water.

"Behold!" Selwyn said, pointing. "Is that the Island of
Procrastination?"

Nearly a mile downstream, a dark projection of land rose
above the surface of the water. Even from such a distance
Josiah could see that the island was rocky and bare. Here

and there, dark, twisted forms towered high into the air, and Josiah surmised that they were giant trees. In the center of the north end, a rocky knoll rose high above the rest of the island. Situated on the knoll in such a way that its inhabitants had a clear view of the entire island, there stood a dark, forbidding castle.

"The Castle of Resistance," Josiah whispered.

"It looks frightening," Gilda said, also whispering.

"I'm sure it is," Josiah replied, "but that's where we'll find Everyman, so that's where we'll go."

"The island must be at least three or four furlongs from the shore," Selwyn said. "How will we ever get out there?"

"I don't know yet," Josiah replied. "Let's get closer."

They hiked downstream. As they came abreast of the Island of Procrastination, they stopped and stared in fascination at the sinister castle. Josiah felt his heart pound with anticipation. Within hours their mission could climax in triumph or disaster. He let out his breath slowly.

"Compassion suggested a surprise visit," Selwyn said, studying the ominous castle, "but that's going to be almost impossible. Look at that place! Did you ever see a fortress so heavily guarded?" Numerous guard towers rose above the castle curtains. Countless sentries walked the battlements, carefully patrolling every section of the walls.

"Behold the front gate," Gilda suggested. "An entire army could never batter their way through that."

"So a surprise attack on the castle is impossible and a direct assault is just as bad," Josiah said with a wry grin. "What do you suggest?"

His companions were silent.

All three studied the situation in silence for several long minutes.

Finally, Selwyn spoke. "I don't see how we can even get across the river. Look at that current! We could never hope to swim across. But even if we could, the currents would bash us against the rocky shore of the island."

"Aye, it does appear to be impossible," Gilda declared.

"Nay, it is not impossible," Josiah reasoned, "or King Emmanuel would never have sent us on this mission in the first place."

"Well, I don't see how we're going to get across," Selwyn stated, "or how we're going to gain entrance to the castle if we do make it across."

"Trust in King Emmanuel," Josiah replied.

Just then Gilda spotted a small craft bobbing against the rocky shore thirty or forty paces downstream. "Behold, a little fishing boat." She dashed down to it. "The oars are in it," she called. "We can take it across to the island."

Selwyn and Josiah hurried to her. "Let's take the boat across to the island," the girl suggested again.

"It looks awfully old," Josiah observed. "This boat is ready to fall apart."

"But it's not that far to the island and back," Gilda argued. "Let's do it."

Josiah hesitated.

"Now who's the timid one?" Gilda teased.

Selwyn spoke up. "It doesn't look safe to me either."

"But we didn't come all this way for nothing," the girl persisted. "I don't see any way across to the island unless we take this boat. Come on—let's do it."

"The boat doesn't belong to us," her brother replied. "We can't borrow it without asking."

"The painter isn't tied," Josiah pointed out. "It's just snagged between those two rocks. I think this boat drifted down from someplace else and got stuck here. If that's true, then it doesn't belong to anybody around here, and it wouldn't be wrong for us to use it."

"Perhaps King Emmanuel provided it for us to use," Gilda remarked. "I think we ought to try it."

"Gilda, you sit in front," Josiah decided. "Selwyn and I will row. It will take both of us to make headway against that current."

In no time at all the little boat was slowly making its way out toward the Island of Procrastination. Just as Josiah had feared, the treacherous currents worked against them, swinging the bow of the boat first one way and then another as if determined to prevent them from reaching the island. The boys rowed fiercely, throwing their full strength into the oars and doing their best to steer a straight course toward the forbidding island.

"Uh oh, we have a problem," Gilda called a moment later.

"What is it?" her brother asked impatiently.

"There's a lot of water down under my feet," the girl answered. "I think we sprang a leak!"

Josiah glanced over his shoulder. "She's right," he told Selwyn. "Row faster!" Both princes rowed with all their might.

"It's coming in faster!" Gilda wailed. "I think it's getting worse. Josiah! Selwyn! Turn the boat around! We're not going to make it! We're sinking!"

Just then Josiah felt a cold wetness around his shins and looked down. Dirty river water sloshed around in the bottom of the boat, so deep that it had flowed over the tops of his boots. "Selwyn!" he cried, "let's turn the boat around! Gilda's right—we're sinking!"

The boys swiftly turned the boat around and rowed frantically for shore. "Hurry, hurry!" Gilda encouraged. "We can make it! We—"

Just then, the hull of the little craft seemed to split wide open and water gushed in like a flood. The bow dropped straight down. The stern lifted above the water, raising Selwyn and Josiah up in the air. The craft hesitated for just an instant, and then dropped like a rock. Within seconds, the little boat had disappeared beneath the surging currents and King Emmanuel's three emissaries found themselves struggling in the foul water.

Chapter Twelve

The boat had sunk quickly. Like a waterfowl diving in search of edible roots, the little craft had simply dropped her nose and plunged beneath the surface of the swift flowing river. In an instant, her three passengers found themselves floundering in the water.

"Help!" Princess Gilda cried. "Save me!"

I can't swim with my armor on, Prince Josiah thought at the moment the water closed over his head. *I'll sink like a rock!*

Josiah lunged upward, filling his lungs with precious air. The weight of his armor pulled him down again. His boots struck the muddy bottom and he found to his amazement that he could stand. The water came barely to his shoulders. The filthy water swirled and surged around him, but the weight of his armor kept him firmly planted in one spot, enabling him to stand against the current. He reached out to Gilda, who struggled just a yard away. "Gilda! Grab my hand!"

The terrified girl seized his outstretched fingers.

Step by step, Josiah slowly slogged toward the riverbank, pulling Gilda with him. Each time he took a step, the muck and mire in the riverbed tugged at his boots as if determined to stop him, but he fought against it. When he had pulled Gilda to the relative safety of waist deep water he looked around. "Where's Selwyn?"

"I'm right here," Selwyn called, and Josiah looked over to see his friend just paces away. "Thanks for helping Gilda."

"Look at you two," Josiah teased, as he and his companions stepped from the River of Consequence. "You look like a pair of drowned rats!"

"Well, Josiah, we tried Gilda's idea," Selwyn said, throwing a broad grin in his sister's direction. "Do you have any better ideas as to how to reach the island?"

Gilda opened her mouth to defend herself, hesitated, and then burst into laughter. Selwyn joined in and then Josiah. All three howled with laughter. "If only Sir Wisdom could see us now!" Josiah exclaimed.

"You should have seen your face when the boat went down," Gilda told her brother. "You had just turned and looked over your shoulder to see what was happening, and the boat fell apart right at that moment. The look on your face—" She bent over with laughter, unable to continue.

"So what do we do now?" Selwyn asked, when the moment of hilarity had passed. "We all look like drowned rats, and we still don't know how to get across to the island."

"Is the parchment with Everyman's pardon all right?" Gilda interrupted.

Josiah reached inside the wet fabric of his doublet and withdrew his book. Opening the volume, he pulled out the precious document. To his relief, the pardon was undamaged. "It's all right," he said, with a sigh of relief. "My clothes are soaked, but my book and the pardon are both all right."

"Something's moving in the reeds downstream," Selwyn said suddenly. "Look!"

Josiah spun around. Less than a furlong downstream,

something large was indeed moving in the reeds along the riverbank. As the trio watched, a flat-bottomed boat slid slowly out from the bank and headed toward the island. Standing high in the stern was an old man poling the craft against the current with all his might. "It's a ferry!" Josiah cried. "He could take us out to the island."

Josiah dashed downstream toward the ferry, which was still just yards from shore. "Wait," he called. "Wait, sir! We need your help!"

The old man heard his cries, turned around and gazed at him for a moment, and then reversed direction and brought the craft back to the shore. "Is there a problem, my lord?"

"We need to get to the island," Josiah told him breathlessly. "Can you take us?"

"Certainly, my lord. I'd be happy to help."

The young prince hesitated. "What is the charge, sir?"

The old man shook his head. "No charge." He looked the three young people over. "But I can hardly take you in the condition you are now, you understand. You're all wet. You'd drip this foul river water all over my boat! Why don't you get cleaned up a bit and then come back tomorrow?"

"But we need to go now," Josiah reasoned.

The man looked at the sky. "It's going to be dark in little more than an hour anyway, my lord. Tomorrow would be far better."

ᘒ

Hours later the three young people sat motionless around a campfire, quietly watching the glowing figures that seemed to leap and dance and frolic within the flames. They had made camp in a small clearing deep within the woods, far from the watchful eyes of any sentries who might be walking the battlements atop the Castle of Resistance. It just would not do for the enemy to spot their campfire.

Josiah stirred the embers with a stick. Thousands of glowing sparks shot skyward like energetic fireflies. "The Castle of Resistance looked so... so solid and so strong, didn't it?" Selwyn remarked. "The way it sat upon that steep hill overlooking the island... the towers seemed so tall, and the gates so strong, and... I just don't know how we're ever going to get in."

"Aye, and we also have to get back out," Josiah added.

"It makes me feel nervous and fearful just looking at it," Selwyn continued. "I know that King Emmanuel sent us; and I know that this assignment is from him and that we should trust him, but—well, this afternoon I just felt so helpless and afraid every time I looked at the castle."

"I feel the same way just thinking about it now," Gilda confessed.

Josiah stirred the embers once more, and again the sparks leaped upward.

"The ferryman will take us across to the island tomorrow, now that our clothes are dry and cleaned up a bit," Selwyn continued, "but how are we going to get inside the castle? You saw the sentries. There must be scores of them."

"Compassion advised us to try a surprise attack," Josiah said thoughtfully, "but I don't see how we possibly could, since the castle is so well guarded. I wonder—"

Selwyn studied him. "You have that look on your face again."

"What look?"

"That look you always get when you're hatching some crazy idea. Do you have a plan?"

Josiah shook his head. "Not really. Nothing that would work, anyway." He yawned and rubbed his eyes. "Let's get some sleep, shall we? Tomorrow's going to be quite a day."

After saying good night to each other, Gilda, Josiah, and Selwyn crawled into the three little lean-tos that they had fashioned from branches, twigs and sticks. Within moments, all three were sound asleep.

The next morning found them hurrying through a simple breakfast taken from their packs of provisions. They carefully doused and covered their fire, used additional branches to camouflage their lean-tos, and then headed for the river. "The ferryman said that he would take us across today," Selwyn told the others, "but I still don't know how we will get inside the castle walls."

"We challenged the guards at the Dungeon of Condemnation where the miller was imprisoned," Gilda piped up, "and they let us in. Wouldn't that work at the castle?"

"We could try that," her brother replied, "but I don't think it would work here."

"Why not?"

"Did you see how heavily fortified this castle was? The gate was closed, the portcullis was down, and the walls were swarming with sentries. Unless I'm mistaken, I even saw pots of boiling water on top of the battlements! They were ready and waiting for an attack. There's a reason it's called 'The Castle of Resistance.' No, I don't think we can just walk up and challenge the guards like we did at the other dungeon."

"So what are our plans?" the girl asked.

"The first step is getting across to the island," Josiah told her. "After that we'll figure out how to get inside the castle."

They reached the River of Consequence at that point to find the old ferryman sitting on the riverbank beside his boat. He had a cane pole in his hand, and he was fishing. As they approached, he looked up and saw them and then pulled in his line.

"We're ready, sir," Josiah told him. "Can you take us across to the island?"

"This isn't the best day to go, my lord," the ferryman replied.

"Why not, sir? Time is of the essence. We are on an important mission for His Majesty, King Emmanuel. We must go today."

"I figured that you were on an errand for the King," the old man said, putting a fresh worm on his hook. He flipped the line out into the water. "I also figured that you would be in a bit of a hurry today. But the timing just isn't right, my lord. Tomorrow would be much better."

Josiah was frustrated at the delay. "But why? We must go today!"

The old man shook his head. "I wouldn't do it today, my lord."

"Why not, sir?"

"Look at the Castle of Resistance—see all the sentries upon the walls? They doubled the guard today, which they do from time to time. The castle is on 'high alert', and the guards will be all fidgety and nervous. Nay, my lord, tomorrow would be much better."

Josiah sighed. "But will you take us today?"

The ferryman shook his head again. "Not today, my lord. Let's make the crossing tomorrow."

Selwyn spoke up. "Prince Josiah is right, sir. We must make the crossing today. We're on a mission of life and death, and time is running out. We really must go today."

"Then swim the river," the old man told him with a sneer,

"if you're in that much of a hurry! But I'm not going anywhere near the Castle of Resistance today or any day that the castle is on high alert. If you're going to make the trip today, my lords, you'll do it without me."

"Then lend us your boat," Josiah suggested. "We'll make the crossing by ourselves."

The old ferryman laughed at him. "The currents out there would capsize this boat in an instant if you don't know what you're doing. Nay, you'll have to wait for me, my lord. We'll go tomorrow."

Gilda, Selwyn and Josiah were frustrated as they walked back to their hideaway camp. "So we have to wait another whole day," Josiah said in exasperation. "What if the Castle of Resistance is on high alert tomorrow? We'll have to wait yet another day."

"He talked as if the high alert thing would be over tomorrow," Gilda said thoughtfully. "Be patient. We'll go tomorrow. This will give us some time to come up with a plan for getting inside the castle."

"I can't take you today either, my lords and my lady," the old man said the next day, slowly shaking his head. "I'm sorry."

"But you promised!" Josiah exclaimed. "This is the third day. We *have* to go today!"

"I'm sorry, my lord, but I just can't do it."

"Why not?" Selwyn demanded.

"The wind is mighty rough today, my lord. Look at the river. See all the whitecaps? I'd never attempt a crossing on a day like this. We'd capsize before we'd gone a hundred paces."

Josiah stared across the water. "It doesn't look all that rough to me."

"I've been a river man all my life, my lord. Trust me; the river is extremely treacherous today. Seldom do I ever see it this rough. Be patient just one more day, and I'll take you across tomorrow. I promise."

Prince Josiah was in a bad mood as he and his companions walked back to camp. "We're losing valuable time," he fumed. "It's one excuse after another."

"He promised that he would take us tomorrow," Princess Gilda said quietly.

Josiah snorted. "Tomorrow he'll just have another excuse. He won't be feeling well, or his boat will need repairing, or..." He stopped suddenly and clapped his hand to his mouth as a startling thought occurred to him.

Selwyn noticed. "What's the matter?"

"You know something?" Josiah replied slowly. "I don't think he ever intends to take us. It's one excuse after another. You know what I think? I think he's purposely trying to delay us. He's keeping us from reaching Everyman with the pardon!"

Selwyn frowned. "Why would he want to do that?"

Josiah shrugged. "Perhaps he's an agent for Argamor."

Selwyn shook his head. "I don't think so, Josiah. He seems willing enough. He's not even going to charge us."

"But he hasn't actually taken us across, has he? Mark my words—he won't take us tomorrow, either. He'll have another excuse why we have to wait another day." Josiah looked earnestly at his friend. "Selwyn, in another few days Everyman will be out of time. We *have* to cross that river tomorrow! Even if we have to swim."

"Nay, we could never swim across, Josiah."

"Well, we have to do something. Time is running out."

"There's not even a hint of a breeze today and there are fewer guards than usual atop the castle walls," Josiah told Selwyn and Gilda as they hurried down to the River of Consequence on the morning of the fourth day. He glanced up at the sky. The day was bright and sunny with a few fluffy clouds that hung low over the island. "What kind of an excuse do you think he will come up with today—it's too cloudy?"

"Maybe today he'll take us," Gilda offered hopefully.

Josiah shook his head. "I don't think so. Just wait—he'll have some excuse."

The ferryman looked up as they approached. "Good morning, my lords and my lady."

"Are you going to take us across today, sir?" Selwyn asked.

An apologetic look appeared on the man's face. "I'm sorry, my lords and my lady, I really am, but I just can't do it today. My joints are aching something fierce today, and I can scarcely move. I feel all weak and trembly. If we were to get out in the middle of that current, I couldn't even steer the vessel. Please accept my humble apologies."

"But you told us that you would take us today," Gilda reminded him. "You promised!"

"I know I did, my lady, and I'm very sorry about the whole thing."

Josiah stepped forward. "By what name are you called, sir?"

The ferryman looked startled. "My name, my lord? What does my name matter?"

"Tell me your name," Josiah insisted.

"I'm just a humble ferryman trying to be of service, my lord. My name is not important."

"Sir, I must learn your name," Josiah demanded.

The ferryman mumbled something that Josiah couldn't hear.

"Louder, sir. I must know your name."

The old man looked defiant. "My name is of no consequence, my lord, but if you must know, my name is Delay."

"Just as I thought!" Josiah replied angrily. Without another word, he turned and strode quickly up the riverbank. Gilda and Selwyn hurried to catch up with him.

"What was that all about?" Selwyn asked moments later as they entered the clearing where their camp was located.

"Don't you see?" Josiah replied, clenching his fists in frustration. "Delay is an agent of Argamor! He never intended to ferry us across the River of Consequence; his purpose was to delay us. He gave us one excuse after another why we should wait one more day to take King Emmanuel's pardon to Everyman. He was hoping to delay us until finally Everyman would be out of time and be executed."

"We lost three entire days because of him," Selwyn observed.

Josiah nodded. "I just hope we're not too late already."

Just then the trio heard a loud crashing coming from the underbrush. Gilda grabbed Josiah's arm. "Something's coming, Josiah. Something big!"

Chapter Thirteen

Prince Josiah and his two companions stood nervously watching the dense foliage. The crashing sound came closer. They could see branches moving, but still could not see the cause of the disturbance. "W-what is it?" Gilda asked, fearfully clutching Josiah's arm in a painful grip.

"I don't know, but whatever it is, it must be huge," Josiah replied. He pried Gilda's fingers loose from his arm. The branches parted at that moment to reveal the hideous black face of an avral.

"It's Leidra!" Gilda said, with a shriek of joy. "Josiah, it's Leidra!" She ran forward to greet the huge caterpillar.

Selwyn looked quizzically at Josiah. "Is that Leidra?"

The young prince shook his head. "I can't tell. Avrals all look alike to me."

The avral raised the front portion of her body in the air and began to rub her rubbery face against Gilda's shoulder. Both boys laughed. "It's Leidra." Josiah and Selwyn hurried forward and all three young people vigorously stroked and petted the huge creature's soft, silky body. Leidra wriggled with delight. Her face contorted and twisted rapidly.

"Leidra, we need your help," Gilda told the creature, gently stroking the fine silver hair that covered most of the pale green body. "We must get across to the Island of Procrastination to deliver the King's pardon to Everyman. He's in the dungeon beneath the Castle of Resistance. But we have no way to cross the river! Can you help us?"

Selwyn laughed at her. "Gilda, she's a caterpillar! What can she do?"

Gilda was hurt by his ridicule. "Sir Wisdom said that avrals can understand nearly everything we say, Selwyn."

"She might understand you, but what can she do? She's a caterpillar."

Leidra lowered her head to the ground and crawled away rapidly. Gilda turned on her brother. "Now look what you have done!" she said accusingly. "You have hurt her feelings."

The avral stopped on the far side of the clearing and raised her upper body into the air. A piercing whistle blasted through the morning air, incredibly loud and shrill. The sound echoed across the hillside. A second whistle immediately sounded, and then a third. Gilda looked at her brother in astonishment. "Is Leidra doing that?"

Selwyn shrugged. "I think so."

The three young ambassadors stood curiously watching the avral. Moments later the sound of the whistle sounded three more times— long shrill blasts that echoed across the hillside. "It *is* Leidra! But why is she doing that?"

"I don't know, Gilda. Wait and see what happens."

From somewhere far in the distance came a sound unlike anything the three young people had ever heard. The noise was like sharp, quick claps of thunder in rapid succession. As Josiah, Gilda, and Selwyn waited anxiously, the sound grew louder and louder until it had become a deafening roar. Gilda put her hands over her ears.

Selwyn pointed skyward. "Look! That's—that's incredible!"

Josiah looked up. Huge, golden creatures resembling butter-flies with enormous, colorful wings dropped from the clouds to hover above the hillside. The three young people stared upward in fascination.

"Butterflies as big as houses," Selwyn exclaimed in awe.

"I've never seen anything like it!" Josiah said softly.

"They're lepidoptera," Gilda said. "Leidra called them here."

There were fifteen or twenty of the breath-taking creatures. Their shimmering, transparent wings beat in unison as they hovered, flashing dazzling rainbows of color and light. As they dropped slowly toward the earth, the downdraft from their gi-gantic wings made the branches of the trees around the clear-ing dance and shake as if they were being pounded by a violent windstorm.

"Thirty-foot wingspans," Selwyn said quietly, "just like Sir Wisdom said."

"Their wings look like enormous stained glass windows," Gilda observed, "only much, much prettier."

"Sir Wisdom called them 'the most magnificent creatures in all Terrestria.' "

As the young people watched, three of the lepidopteras dropped down and alighted on the grass while the others con-tinued to hover nearly a hundred feet in the air. The three magnificent creatures on the ground slowly opened and closed their huge, iridescent wings repeatedly.

"What are they doing?" Gilda asked in a whisper, awed by the spectacle of the giant butterflies.

"Sh-h! Just watch," Selwyn whispered back.

The three lepidopteras continued to slowly open and close their magnificent wings. The rest of the brilliant creatures remained in the air, hovering about a hundred feet above the ground. "Why are they just staying there?" Gilda asked, alternately watching the three on the ground and then the group in the air. "It looks like they're waiting for something!"

Josiah was startled by a sudden pressure against his back. He turned around. "Leidra! What are you doing?"

The giant caterpillar had raised her head up to a level just above Josiah's waist and was pushing firmly against the back of his doublet. Josiah was uncomfortable with the situation and he pushed back, hoping that the friendly creature would leave him alone. But Leidra continued to press against his back, pushing so hard that he was finally compelled to step forward. As soon as he did, she moved forward with him and pushed again. He took another step. "Leidra! Leave me alone!"

"She likes you," Gilda told him.

"Aye, well, I wish she would show it in some other way," Josiah replied. "I don't like this!" At that moment, the pressure abruptly ceased as the big avral took her head away from Josiah's back. The young prince let out a sigh of relief. "That's better, Leidra."

But in the next instant Josiah found himself hoisted into the air. Gripping the back of his cloak in her rubbery mouth, Leidra carried him straight to one of the waiting lepidopteras and deposited him on the abdomen of the huge creature. The young prince tried immediately to scramble back down, but Leidra was directly behind him, blocking his way.

Selwyn came running forward. "Josiah! She wants you to ride it!"

Josiah was thunderstruck at the idea. "Ride a lepidoptera?"

It was Gilda who caught on first. "Josiah! Selwyn!" she shouted, dashing forward. "This is our way across to the Island of Procrastination! Leidra called them for us. There are three lepidopteras waiting here, and three of us. We're each supposed to climb aboard one of them and ride across to the island."

Josiah turned and looked at Leidra. Her huge head was bobbing up and down and her mouth parts were wriggling energetically. Her whole body twisted and wiggled. "I think you're right, Gilda," he called. "Leidra seems to like the idea." A bit timid about the situation, he nevertheless crawled forward and sat on the thorax of the huge creature. Wrapping his legs around the lepidoptera's middle, he leaned forward and grasped the powerful muscles attaching the massive wings to the body.

The huge wings immediately began to beat rapidly and the lepidoptera lifted slowly into the air. The young prince felt a breathtaking surge of fear and excitement. To his surprise, the roar of the tremendous wings was not nearly as loud as he had expected. He turned and looked behind him and then realized that he was already sixty or seventy feet in the air. "Climb on!" he called down to his companions, hoping they would be able to hear him above the noise of the mighty wings. "You're going to be left behind!"

He watched as Gilda and her brother scrambled aboard the two waiting lepidopteras. In no time at all the three spectacular creatures had reached the altitude where the rest of the group was hovering. The noise of the mighty wings increased as the entire band of huge butterflies began to climb higher. Josiah looked down and discovered that they were already several hundred feet in the air. He tightened his grip.

"How much higher do these things fly?" Selwyn called.

Josiah turned and looked at him. Selwyn's face was deathly white and he looked as if he was going to be sick. "I don't know," Josiah called back, "but isn't this a splendid way to travel?"

Josiah looked down. Far below, the River of Consequence appeared as a narrow, brown ribbon winding its way through a carpet of green. He spotted the Island of Procrastination, which from this altitude looked to be the size of a coin. The castle was hardly more than a dot. He took a deep breath. The Land of Unbelief looked so much different from up here.

At that moment the band of lepidopteras entered the clouds. Josiah was abruptly surrounded by a swirling white mist so thick that he could see just a few feet. Suddenly it seemed that he was all alone on the back of the giant lepidoptera. His two companions had vanished along with the rest of the magnificent winged creatures. "Selwyn," he called, "are you there?"

"I'm here," came the answering reply, "but I can't see you."

"Where's Gilda?"

"I'm right here, too."

"Where are they taking us?" Selwyn called.

"We were over the River of Consequence when we entered the clouds," Josiah replied. "I think they're taking us to the island."

Just then the huge lepidoptera raised its mighty wings and held them motionless. Josiah felt a strange, spinning sensation and the mists swirled around him. Although he could see nothing except the milky whiteness of the clouds around him, Josiah sensed that he and the giant butterfly were spiraling rapidly downward. Suddenly the lepidoptera dropped out of the clouds and Josiah saw that the Castle of Resistance was directly below him.

As the giant butterfly dropped from the sky, the castle grew larger and larger. It seemed to be rushing up to meet him. Moments later they landed noiselessly within the castle walls. Josiah heard a soft whooshing sound and looked over just in time to see two other lepidopteras come spiraling down to land in the same manner. Josiah scrambled down from the back of the huge creature. Selwyn and Gilda came running to meet him.

Raising their huge, colorful wings, the three lepidopteras rose majestically into the air and thundered toward the heavens. Within seconds they had disappeared into the clouds. "Wasn't that incredible?" Gilda exclaimed in delight. "We actually got to ride them!"

The three young people found themselves standing within a large courtyard filled with gloom and dark shadows. The castle walls loomed high above them, stern and imposing. High on the battlements, a number of soldiers patrolled the castle walls, alert and watchful. Josiah's heart pounded with anticipation. *We're actually inside the Castle of Resistance,* he told himself. *We made it! Now to find Everyman.*

Hearing the sound of running feet, he looked up to see numerous guards dashing down several flights of stairs that led from the sentrywalk to the courtyard. "Hide!" Josiah urged Selwyn and Gilda. "The guards are coming! They saw the lepidopteras!"

The three young people looked around frantically. Spotting no ideal hiding place, Josiah dashed across the courtyard and scrambled into a tangle of shrubbery beside the stairs. Selwyn and Gilda joined him. Hidden in the shadows, they waited anxiously.

"There were at least three of them," a gruff voice said suddenly, and the three young people peered out to see two guards standing just paces from their hiding place. "They came this way and they couldn't have gotten far. We'll find them!"

"Who are these trespassers and from whence did they come? What were those giant winged creatures on which they rode? I've never seen anything like it."

"I know not who they are or where they came from, and I have never before seen creatures such as they rode. I rather suspect that they were sent by our adversary."

The second guard let out a gasp of dismay. "King Emmanuel?"

His companion nodded. "None other. But we will find these intruders and take off their heads."

"Aye, but if they have been sent by King Emmanuel—"

"It matters not who sent them; they are intruders and must be dealt with harshly." Swinging his sword fiercely, the soldier lopped off a branch of the very bush beneath which the three young ambassadors were hiding. "Lord Argamor would have it no other way."

Josiah's heart pounded with fear.

"We will search every inch of this wretched castle until we find them," the first guard vowed. "They can't escape." After this brief exchange, the guards moved away. Moments later, the sound of numerous feet told Josiah that several guards were searching the courtyard.

"Josiah!" Selwyn's voice was right in his ear, startling him and nearly causing him to cry out. "Josiah, there's a door in the wall right behind this bush. If we can open it and slip through without the guards seeing us, perhaps we can find a better hiding place. If they search the courtyard very carefully they're going to find us here almost immediately."

Before Josiah had a chance to reply, the sound of rusty hinges told him that Selwyn had already succeeded in opening the door. "Josiah! In here!"

The young prince crawled from beneath the bush and slipped quickly through the narrow doorway. Gilda was right behind him, and Selwyn closed the door. As their eyes grew accustomed to the dim light, they could see that they were standing in a gloomy chamber with a high, vaulted ceiling. Row after row of dusty objects sat on shelves upon the walls; the large, oaken table before them was piled high with mounds of dust-covered fabric. Large wooden racks in the center of the room held an assortment of longbows, swords, and battleaxes.

Gilda picked up a garment from the table, raising a cloud of dust that made them all cough. She held the garment up to the light from the grimy window. "It's a uniform!" she exclaimed. "A guard's uniform."

Selwyn plucked one of the large items from a shelf on the wall. "A helmet," he said softly, almost as if he were in awe. "And there are breastplates, and shields, and... Josiah, we're in the castle armory."

"This is the way to elude the guards!" Gilda said excitedly, brushing away some of the dust so that she could better see the garment she held. "We'll dress out in their uniforms and armor. We'll look like Argamor's guards, instead of King Emmanuel's ambassadors. We can then go anywhere in the Castle of Resistance, and we'll look like we belong here. No one will know who we are, and no one will challenge us!"

"Aye, I think it will work," Josiah replied, after thinking it through for a moment. "We can tuck your hair up under your helmet, and if you keep your head down, no one will see that you are a girl. We just might pass for guards. I think it will work."

The trio quickly searched the castle armory for uniforms and armor that would fit. The air was soon filled with dust, making it difficult to see or breathe. "Here's a small helmet," Selwyn told Gilda. "Try it on."

"And here's a breastplate that will fit me," Josiah said quietly, holding the item of armor against his chest, "but it needs cleaned up a bit."

"Here's a uniform that's small enough to fit me," Gilda said.

"I'll try to find ones that will fit both of you."

Selwyn paused and held up one hand. "Listen." The sounds from outside the armory told them that the guards were still searching the courtyard. "They would have found us for certain if we had not found our way in here," he quietly told the others. "But once we have our disguises on, we can go anywhere in the castle."

The helmet slipped from his hands and fell to the stone floor with a clatter that echoed throughout the armory. Selwyn and his companions stood still for several seconds, listening intently, but no guards rushed to the armory to check out the disturbance. Selwyn bent over to pick up the helmet. "Sorry."

Just then, the armory door opened abruptly. Two huge guards with drawn swords stood framed in the doorway.

Chapter Fourteen

The two young princes and the princess stood frozen with fear as the two brawny guards strode into the darkened chamber. "The sound came from the armory," a gruff voice growled. "The intruders are in here somewhere!"

Prince Josiah thought his heart would stop. Moving slowly and carefully, he and his companions crept noiselessly behind the racks of weapons. Hardly daring to breathe, they dropped to their knees on the cold stone floor. A hard, cold sensation of fear tied Josiah's stomach in knots. Every nerve in his tense body seemed to leap and shudder.

One of the guards sneezed. "It's so dusty in here I can't see a thing." He sneezed again.

His companion held up one hand. "Listen," he whispered.

Two more guards appeared in the doorway just then. "Find something?"

"Aye, they're hiding in here. We heard a noise."

Josiah's fear increased and his heart pounded faster. In just a moment or two their hiding place would be discovered and the entire garrison of enemy knights would come storming into the armory. No matter how valiantly he and Selwyn and Gilda fought, he knew that they could not possibly hope to defeat so powerful an enemy force. Argamor's knights would win, and the pardon would never reach Everyman.

At that moment a shelf bracket came loose from the wall. An entire row of steel helmets tumbled to the floor, bouncing and scattering about the armory with such a clatter that it sounded as if the castle itself was collapsing. A score of knights came running to check out the disturbance. "What is all this row?" an authoritative voice called sternly.

"Timidity heard a noise and thought that he had discovered the intruders in the armory, sire," another voice replied.

"Did you search the armory?"

"The noise was just helmets falling from the shelves, sire."

Scornful laughter filled the passageway outside the armory. "You call yourselves knights?" the officer sneered. "You're acting like a bunch of doddering old women, afraid of your own shadows." His tone became mean and ugly. "Now get on with the search, you pack of spineless squires! The intruders are not in the west bailey, so search the east wing and the east bailey. I want those intruders found! Get moving!"

Thoroughly embarrassed and humiliated by the officer's tirade, the guards lost no time in making themselves scarce. The officer growled his frustration as he closed the door to the armory. Josiah let out his breath in a long sigh of relief.

"Let's get dressed in these uniforms and then stay here a few minutes until the search dies down," Selwyn suggested. "Once we look like the castle guards I think we can safely go anywhere, but we might as well not take any more chances than we have to."

"How do I look?" Gilda asked a few moments later. "Will I pass for a castle guard?"

Selwyn looked up from his task of tightening the straps on the breastplate he had borrowed. "A little on the small side, perhaps," he replied with a smile, "but I think it will do. Just remember to keep your head down if we pass anybody in the corridors."

Josiah looked her over. "Your own mother wouldn't recognize you." He slipped one of the guards' helmets into place where just moments before his own helmet had rested. "I think we're all ready."

Selwyn laughed. "I think any one of us could pass for one of Argamor's guards."

Josiah grabbed his arm. "What did you say?"

Selwyn gave him a puzzled look. "I just said that we look like Argamor's men."

The idea troubled Josiah. "Argamor is our adversary!" he declared. "He's the sworn enemy of our Lord and Master, King Emmanuel." He lifted the helmet from his head. "I am a child of the King. I cannot wear the uniform of His Majesty's enemy. I cannot look like one of Argamor's men."

"Aye, but it's just for a few minutes," Selwyn argued. "It's just a disguise to get past the castle guards. We'll only wear it until we reach the Dungeon of Condemnation and deliver the pardon to Everyman."

Josiah set the helmet on the table. He shook his head. "Nay, I cannot do it. I simply cannot wear the uniform of the enemy. I'm a child of the King, and I cannot in any way be associated with his enemies."

"It's for a good cause," Selwyn persisted. "We're only doing it so that we can get past the guards and deliver the pardon to Everyman."

"If it's wrong for me to wear the uniform of the enemy, then it's wrong for me to wear it even to try to accomplish something good. It is never right to do wrong in order for an opportunity to do right." Josiah began to unstrap the breastplate.

"Wouldn't it be better for us to go openly, as children of His Majesty, King Emmanuel, trusting him for the victory?"

Selwyn and Gilda thought it over. "Aye, you're right," Selwyn said at last. "As children of King Emmanuel, it would never do for us to wear the uniform of Argamor. We must be careful to do nothing that would associate us with his forces. Let us go unafraid to be recognized as children of the King." Within moments the young ambassadors had removed the guards' uniforms and armor and were once again proudly arrayed in the colors of their King.

Josiah cautiously opened the armory door. "This is the moment we've been waiting for," he said eagerly. "In just a short time we will deliver the King's pardon to Everyman." He drew his sword. "Let's go."

"Watch for the guards," Selwyn warned, drawing his own weapon. "We must be alert. Argamor's forces will do their best to stop us." Gilda drew her sword.

Alert and watchful, they crept cautiously down the darkened corridor. Before long they came to a staircase that spiraled down into the darkened heart of the castle. "It goes down," Josiah pointed out. "Let's follow it. Perhaps it will lead us to the dungeon where Everyman is held."

The stairs led down one level and opened out to a huge chamber with elegant furnishings. "Keep going," Josiah suggested. "This is not it." The trio followed the stairs down one more level and found themselves in a darkened chamber. A flickering torch on the wall illuminated a small area, but they could not see the far wall.

"It's awfully dark down here," Gilda remarked, taking the torch from the wall. "We need this." Within moments, the torch sputtered and went out. "Now what do we do?" she asked plaintively. "It's too dark to see our way without it."

Josiah held his sword against his side until it transformed into the book. He opened the volume and the pages began to glow with a bright white light. "The King's words will guide us." Selwyn and Gilda quickly followed his example.

Following the light from the glowing volumes, Gilda, Selwyn, and Josiah crossed the chamber. At the far end they found three corridors at right angles to each other. "Which one do we take?" Gilda asked aloud.

Josiah held his book high as he turned toward the corridor on the left. The light from the book dimmed noticeably. "That's not it," he said. He held the volume toward the center corridor and the pages dimmed even more. When he held it toward the corridor to the right, the pages glowed brightly. "This way."

"The book will lead us right to Everyman!" Selwyn said excitedly. "We should have thought of that before."

Following the light from the book, the three young people made their way deeper and deeper into the Castle of Resistance. The glowing pages led them on a winding course through one darkened corridor after another, up one stairway and down another, passing through large chambers and small. Finally, they found themselves following a long, narrow corridor that angled sharply downward.

"I think we're getting close," Josiah declared.

Gilda pointed. "Look. There's a strange light up ahead."

A faint glimmer of light illuminated the darkness of the corridor ahead. They hurried toward it. As they drew closer, the unusual light grew brighter, glowing and pulsating and changing colors as they watched. "What is it?" Gilda asked in a tiny, trembling voice.

"I have no idea," Josiah replied. "Let's find out."

"The light is not actually in this passageway," Selwyn observed, as they drew closer. "It's coming from a chamber to the right."

Moving slowly and cautiously, the three young people crept around the corner. "Would you look at that!" Josiah exclaimed softly, closing his book and stowing it within his doublet. "I've never seen anything like it. I would not have thought that there was this much wealth in the entire kingdom of Terrestria!"

The chamber before them was enormous, with walls and floor of the purest white marble. Far above their heads, the vaulted ceiling glittered with gold and silver and reflective panels of crystal. In the center of the floor, piled higher than a man's head, was an immense heap of glittering treasure. Enormous gems by the thousands were piled upon the castle floor, interspersed with countless golden coins, pearls, and silver ingots. The remarkable treasure glowed with an extraordinary, pulsating light, which illuminated the entire treasure chamber.

"Would you look at that!" Josiah exclaimed again, awed at the splendid sight before him. "Diamonds the size of my fist! Rubies and emeralds as big as apples! Sapphires bigger than goose eggs!" He crept forward and picked up a huge diamond. The glittering jewel glowed with a brilliant rainbow of fire, casting tiny points of colored light around the room. He held the enormous gem out toward his companions. "Look at this! This diamond must weight at least three pounds!" He glanced at Selwyn. "These jewels are more than two score times as big as the jewels in our Shields of Faith!"

Selwyn picked up an emerald. "To whom does this all belong?" he whispered.

"Look at that sign," Gilda said, pointing to a small, bronze plaque upon the wall close to the chamber entrance. "What does it say?"

Josiah stood on tiptoe to read the inscription. "Welcome to

the Chamber of Temporal Possessions and Pleasures," he read aloud. "The treasure you see is here for the taking. Feel free to indulge yourselves."

"What does that mean?" Gilda asked.

"I think it means that I can keep this diamond!" Josiah exclaimed, eyeing the huge jewel with delight.

"And it means that we can take as much as we want!" Selwyn exulted. He stepped forward and began to select other jewels, stuffing them into his doublet. Within moments his garment bulged until it could not hold another gem.

Gilda fell to her knees and began to gather enormous, lustrous pearls from the glowing pile of gems. "Look at these pearls," she cried with delight. "They're perfect, and each one is as big as a plum!" She spread the skirt of her gown and began to place the huge pearls within it.

"Let's take some of the treasure back to our camp for safekeeping," Selwyn said excitedly. His eyes glittered with a strange light. "We can then come back for more."

Josiah hesitated, still eyeing the glittering diamond he held. "But what about the pardon for Everyman?"

"We can deliver that later," Selwyn replied nonchalantly. "Let's get our share of the treasure first."

"But our purpose in making the trip was to deliver the pardon to Everyman," Josiah argued. "I think we ought to take care of that first and then come back for the treasure. Delivering the pardon is priority."

Selwyn drew a huge, flawless sapphire from within his doublet. The beautiful jewel glowed with an intense blue fire, casting vivid points of blue light across his helmet, face and breastplate as he moved. "Look at this, Josiah!" he exulted, and his eyes glowed with a strange fire of their own. "Look at the size of this!"

He held the jewel overhead as he gazed at it. "Do you know what a sapphire like this is worth? This one jewel would buy a... a whole castle! I have dozens of jewels like this within my doublet! Do you think I'm going to just walk away from a treasure like this? Josiah, an opportunity like this only comes along once in a lifetime, and I'm not going to miss it! Let's gather our share of the treasure first and then come back with the pardon for Everyman."

"What if Everyman runs out of time?" Gilda asked softly. "Sir Faithful told us that this mission requires haste."

"We'll be back within a few hours," Selwyn argued. "Maybe less than that. We'll call the lepidopteras, have them carry us and the treasure across to our camp and then bring us back to deliver the pardon."

"Do you really think that we'll be satisfied with the jewels we can carry in just one trip?" his sister asked quietly. "Once we make one trip, we'll want more and more. You know what Sir Faithful told us: a little bit of wealth never satisfies anyone; they always want more." She turned to Josiah with pleading eyes. "Let's deliver the pardon first, Josiah. We can come back later for the treasure."

Josiah eyed the huge diamond in his hand as he thought it through. The rare jewel glowed brilliantly, casting a thousand points of multi-colored light about the room. The young prince could hardly take his eyes from it. Josiah found himself drawn irresistibly to the diamond. He had to have it, and he had to have it now. "Aye, you're right," he said at last to Selwyn. "Let's gather as much treasure as we can carry now. We'll come back later with the pardon for Everyman."

"But what if later is too late?" Gilda asked softly.

Josiah ignored her. "The treasure you see is here for the taking," he said grandly, again reading the placard on the wall.

"Feel free to indulge yourselves."

"What does *temporal* mean?" Gilda asked.

Josiah frowned. "Why do you ask that?"

"The sign says that this is the 'Chamber of Temporal Possessions and Pleasures'. I just wondered what *temporal* means."

"It means 'having to do with time'," Josiah answered impatiently. "Another word that means almost the same thing as *temporal* would be *temporary*. I guess you could say it means something that doesn't last." He turned back to Selwyn. "You have quite a load. Now help me gather my share of the treasure."

"Josiah," Gilda interrupted, "Look at your diamond!"

Josiah stared at the jewel in his hand. The diamond had lost its brilliance and its form and become a shapeless mass of translucent rock. As he watched in dismay, the mass in his hand darkened in color and disintegrated even further. "It's melting!" he cried in alarm. "My diamond is melting!" As he spoke, the shapeless mass turned to gooey liquid and dripped from his fingers onto the marble floor. Josiah stared at his empty hand. "The diamond! It's gone!"

"Look at my sapphire!" Selwyn cried. "The same thing is happening to it!" As the trio watched in consternation, the dazzling blue gem turned a smoky gray color and began to change shape. Sinking into a shapeless mass like a lump of warm butter, it dripped from his hand and spattered on the cold stone floor. The young prince's eyes were filled with horror. The puddle of gray matter began to bubble and boil and then evaporated in a puff of smoke.

Josiah stared at the floor where just moments before the remnants of his diamond had dripped. There was no sign of the jewel; the marble floor was clean. "They don't last!" he cried. "These jewels are worthless—they melt in your hands!"

Selwyn cried out in alarm and clawed at his doublet. Seizing the jewels within his garments, he began to hurl them on the floor as fast as he could. Diamonds, emeralds, rubies and sapphires rolled across the floor, melted into colored puddles, and vaporized into tiny puffs of smoke. The young prince tore open his doublet, allowing the remaining jewels to spill out.

Gilda leaped to her feet, dropping the skirt of her gown and scattering huge pearls everywhere. Like the jewels that Josiah and Selwyn had gathered, the pearls melted and then quickly evaporated, leaving not even a mark on the floor to show that they had ever existed.

"They're worthless!" Josiah cried again. "All worthless! They glitter and sparkle and look so beautiful, but once you have them in your possession they quickly turn to nothing. They're worthless!"

"Aye, they are temporal," Gilda said quietly.

Josiah heard her. "What did you say?"

"Temporal," the girl repeated. "These were temporal pleasures. You said temporal means something that doesn't last. You were right. These jewels didn't last at all."

As Josiah thought about her words, a light suddenly came on. "This 'Chamber of Temporal Possessions and Pleasures' was just another of Argamor's traps," he told Gilda and Selwyn. "He had the treasure chamber put here to distract us from our mission: taking King Emmanuel's pardon to Everyman. He was very nearly successful."

Selwyn stepped quickly from the chamber. "Let us delay no further," he declared. "We must press on and deliver the pardon to Everyman before it is forever too late."

Chapter Fifteen

Prince Josiah and his companions hurried down the dark corridor. The pages of their books glowed brighter and brighter until they were shining with an intense white light that was almost blinding to behold. The cold stone walls of the passageway reflected the light, dispelling the darkness completely. "I think we're getting close," Josiah told the others. "Look how brightly my book is glowing."

Moments later they came to a massive iron door blocking the corridor. Josiah reached out and tried the latch, but it was securely locked. Noticing a small brass plate near the bottom of the door, Gilda knelt for a closer look. "What does it say?" Selwyn asked.

"Fear of Rejection," the young princess read. She looked up questioningly at her two companions. "How do we get past this door? This will keep us from reaching Everyman with the pardon."

Josiah closed his book and swung it briskly, transforming it into a sword. "I know how."

Selwyn put one hand on his arm to stop him. "You can't cut your way through an iron door with a sword," he declared. "I have another idea." Reaching within the pages of his own book, he took out a tiny, golden key.

"The Key of Faith," Josiah said aloud. "Of course." Selwyn inserted the tiny key into the lock and the massive iron door opened easily.

Soon they came to a second iron door. Gilda knelt. "Fear of Ridicule," she read. Selwyn's Key of Faith quickly opened the second barrier.

Moments later they faced a third iron door. "This one is the 'Fear of Saying the Wrong Thing'," Gilda reported. Selwyn's key opened it quickly.

"Fear of Failure," Gilda read, kneeling before a fourth door. "How many more of these doors are there?"

"As long as we have the Key of Faith," her brother replied, "it doesn't really matter." He inserted the key and the door swung open easily. Just beyond the door, both sides of the passageway were flanked by rows of narrow cells. "The Dungeon of Condemnation," Selwyn exclaimed softly. "We've reached it at last!"

The first three cells were empty, but the fourth held a prisoner—a slender, well-groomed man in his late twenties. The man's sandy brown hair was of medium length, clean and shiny; his beard was well-kept. He wore an immaculate green-and-silver striped doublet and silver-gray trunk hose. An elegant cloak of dark green hung about his shoulders. Even his hands were clean and well-manicured. *I wonder who he is,* Josiah thought to himself. *He doesn't look like a prisoner in a dungeon. He seems so out of place here.*

The young prince approached the cell. "Sir, could you help us?"

The prisoner looked up in surprise. "How may I be of assistance, my lords?" He bowed politely to Gilda. "My lady."

"We're looking for a prisoner by the name of Everyman," Josiah told him.

142

"Aye, my name is Everyman, my lord."

"The man we're searching for is named Adam Everyman."

The man's face registered surprise. "My lord, I am Adam Everyman. What is your business with me?"

Gilda gave a little cry of delight. "We found him! We found Everyman!"

Josiah stepped forward eagerly. "Sir, we have a pardon for you. It's signed and sealed by none other than His Majesty, King Emmanuel. Adam Everyman, you are a free man. The King has pardoned you."

Everyman seemed perplexed by the news. "A pardon for me, my lord?"

"Aye, sir," Josiah replied happily. "You do not have to die. King Emmanuel has issued a pardon in your name. You are now a free man!"

The young prince was expecting an outburst of joy and gratitude, but instead, Everyman began to laugh. "There must be some mistake, my lord," he said. Standing to his feet, he drew himself up to his full height, squared his shoulders, and puffed out his chest. "The King's pardon must be for someone else, my lord. I am not a condemned man."

"But it *is* for you, sir," Selwyn blurted, "if your name is Adam Everyman. Your name is on the King's pardon."

Everyman laughed again. "My name is Adam Everyman, to be sure, but there must be a mistake. I need no pardon from the King. I am not a condemned man. I assure you, I face no sentence of death. I do not even deserve to be here, my lords; it is all a slight mistake that will be cleared up shortly." He laughed again. "I would suggest that you give the King's pardon to someone who really needs it."

The three young ambassadors stared at each other in disbelief. This was not the reception that they had anticipated.

Josiah took a deep breath. "King Emmanuel's pardon *is* for you, sir. It has your name on it. His Majesty commissioned us personally to deliver his pardon to you." He reached inside his doublet and pulled out the precious parchment. He handed the document through the bars. "Here, sir, from King Emmanuel himself."

Everyman made no move to take the parchment. He merely laughed.

"Please take it, sir," Gilda pleaded. "Unless you have the King's pardon, they will hang you in just a few days!"

Everyman turned to face her. His eyes were wide with mock fear. "Hang me, my lady? Surely you jest."

"It's true, sir," Selwyn interjected. "My sister is right—you are a condemned man. Unless you receive the King's pardon, they will hang you shortly."

The prisoner threw back his head and laughed heartily. "You don't understand, my lords and my lady. I am *not* a condemned man. I am *not* about to face the gallows! I am here simply by mistake. I assure you—I have committed no crime worthy of imprisonment, much less hanging. You are talking to the wrong man."

The three young people hesitated, uncertain as to what to do or say next. Everyman looked from one to another, easily reading the confusion and dismay on their faces. His expression softened. "Don't feel badly, my lords and my lady," he said quickly. "I appreciate your efforts; I really do. But you brought the pardon to the wrong man. I will be out of here in the next day or two, and I really don't need a pardon from the King."

Josiah unrolled the parchment and held it up to the bars so that Everyman could see it. "Look for yourself, sir. The King's pardon *is* for you; your name is on it."

The prisoner stepped close to the bars and glanced at the

document. "So it is, my lord, so it is. But I assure you; I have committed no deeds worthy of death or imprisonment and therefore do not need a pardon from your King. I am an innocent man, and I shall walk free on my own merit in the next day or two."

"Please take it, sir," Gilda pleaded in a trembling voice. Josiah glanced at her and saw that she was nearly in tears. "King Emmanuel sent us! There is no mistake—the pardon is for you. Unless you receive it, you will die in the next few days. Please, sir, accept the King's pardon!"

Everyman slowly shook his head. "I know you mean well, my lady, but I assure you again—I am not a condemned man. I have committed no crimes. I am as innocent as a newborn babe. Therefore, I do not need your King's pardon. Now I'm sorry that you went through all this trouble just for me, and I do appreciate it, I really do. I thank you. But I really do not need this pardon."

Josiah, Gilda, and Selwyn continued to plead with Everyman to accept the King's pardon. They tried to reason with him, but he refused to listen. Finally, he went so far as to step to the back of his cell, turn his face to the wall, and cover his ears. Everyman was doing his best to make it clear that he was not about to accept the King's pardon.

Gilda began to weep softly. "He won't take it," she whispered to Josiah and Selwyn. "He won't even listen to us. Why would anyone reject a pardon from King Emmanuel?"

"He doesn't see his need," her brother said.

Josiah let out his breath in a long sigh of disappointment and frustration. "Everyman doesn't seem to realize that he has committed crimes against King Emmanuel. He sees himself as a good, innocent man, not as a condemned prisoner who will soon face the gallows."

"Aye, but if he rejects the pardon he is going to die," Gilda sobbed.

Josiah nodded soberly. "I know."

Selwyn let out a sigh. "So what do we do now?"

Josiah shook his head. "I don't know. What else can we do? We can't force him to accept the pardon." He rolled up the parchment and replaced it within his doublet. "Let's make our way back to our camp. Perhaps it would be safer to discuss it there than here in the Castle of Resistance."

Ten minutes later they crouched in the shadows of the castle courtyard. "We made it here safely," Gilda said, "but how do we get out of the castle? And how do we get off the island?"

"We simply call the lepidopteras," her brother told her. "They'll take us back to our camp."

"Call the lepidopteras?" Gilda echoed. "How?"

"Watch," Selwyn replied. Standing to his feet, he put his fingers to his mouth and gave three loud, shrill whistles, much as Leidra had done when she had summoned the beautiful winged creatures to carry them across to the island. The sentries atop the castle walls immediately spun around and carefully scanned the courtyard, but the young prince had already dropped back into his hiding place. Moments later, he stood to his feet and repeated the whistles.

"It didn't work," Gilda complained. "The lepidopteras aren't coming. But look who are—the sentries! They'll find us in no time."

Selwyn just smiled. "Aye, but it did work," he said smugly. "Listen."

Josiah and Gilda paused and listened closely. Sure enough, from somewhere in the heavens came a noise that sounded like rapid claps of distant thunder. "Get ready," Selwyn told them. "They'll be here before we know it!"

At that moment, three enormous lepidopteras came spiraling out of the clouds with wings folded. In an instant they had landed within the courtyard of the castle. The three young people leaped from their hiding place and ran to meet them. As Josiah scrambled aboard the thorax of one of the lepidopteras, he saw the castle sentries rushing down the stairs toward the courtyard.

The lepidopteras raised their mighty, translucent wings and thundered into the air, carrying Selwyn, Gilda, and Josiah with them. Gripping the huge wing muscles, Josiah leaned over and watched as the Castle of Resistance fell away below them, rapidly growing smaller and smaller. He felt a tremendous sense of relief at leaving the castle and at the same time, a deep sense of regret since Everyman had rejected King Emmanuel's pardon. Just then thick clouds obscured the castle from view.

Moments later as the lepidopteras flew back out of the clouds the three young people saw that the band of enormous butterflies now numbered in the hundreds. Winging their way across the heavens, the incredible creatures moved in perfect unison. Rainbows of iridescent color seemed to burst from their magnificent wings to radiate across the sky. The sight was one that Josiah would never forget.

The entire band of lepidopteras circled the camp three times and then three of them dropped down to land lightly upon the grass. The others hovered above the camp with their magnificent wings still flashing rainbows of brilliant color across the sky. Gilda, Josiah, and Selwyn scrambled down. With the thunder of mighty wings, the lepidopteras disappeared into the heavens.

The young people hurried across the meadow to their camp. A tall nobleman was waiting for them. "Sir Wisdom!" Josiah exclaimed, embracing the old man.

"Everyman rejected the King's pardon," Gilda wailed. "We

tried and tried, but we couldn't get him to accept it. Oh, Sir Wisdom, what are we to do? Everyman will soon be executed, and there's nothing that we can do."

The old man tenderly stroked her hair. "King Emmanuel created Everyman with a free will," he said gently. "Everyman must decide for himself if he will receive or reject His Majesty's offer of a free pardon."

"Everyman sees himself as an innocent man who does not need King Emmanuel's pardon," Selwyn explained. "We tried to reason with him, sire. We did our best to show him that he stands condemned and can be executed at any time. But he kept telling us that he was innocent, that his imprisonment is a mistake, and that he will soon be freed on account of his own goodness. He wouldn't listen to us, sire."

Gilda was crying. "He doesn't even realize that he is going to perish."

Sir Wisdom nodded sadly. "Everyman's response is typical of many of the inhabitants of the Land of Unbelief. No one likes to think of himself as guilty, deserving of punishment. It's quite typical to deny the reality of one's guilt—much as Everyman is doing—and blindly hope that one's good deeds will make up for the evil that one has done."

"But King Emmanuel is offering a full pardon!" Josiah exclaimed. "Why will Everyman not receive it?"

"To do so, he must admit his guilt," the old man replied quietly. "His pride keeps him from doing that."

"Even if it sends him to the gallows."

Sir Wisdom nodded. "Aye, so it would seem."

"But how can we persuade him to accept the pardon?" Gilda asked, still in tears. "We have to do something."

"Return to the Castle of Resistance tomorrow and try again," Sir Wisdom suggested. "Warn Everyman again of the judgment that he is facing and again offer him King Emmanuel's pardon. Tomorrow will be his last opportunity to receive the pardon. We can only hope that he will make the right decision."

Chapter Sixteen

The sun was setting on the Land of Unbelief as a mighty host of magnificent lepidopteras dropped from the heavens. They hovered above a small meadow several furlongs from the River of Consequence. Three of the colorful creatures spiraled down from the formation to land upon the grass. Prince Josiah, Prince Selwyn, and Princess Gilda silently climbed down and walked soberly toward the camp.

Sir Wisdom had a cheery fire waiting. "Sit down," he told them gently. "Dinner will be ready in just a moment."

Gilda burst into tears. "We tried so hard, sire! We did our best, but we failed!"

"This was our second trip to the Castle of Resistance," Josiah said quietly, biting his lip in attempt to hold back his own tears, "but Everyman still didn't listen. He... he rejected the King's pardon, sire."

The old nobleman nodded. "I know. Sit down and we'll talk about it while you eat." He knelt by the fire and took a skewer of fish from the flames. The three young ambassadors quietly took seats on the stumps around the fire. "Here, eat," Sir Wisdom said softly, handing a plate of bread and fish to Gilda. "It's been a hard day, but you'll feel better with something in your bellies." He passed two more plates to Josiah and Selwyn.

"We had to fight our way into the dungeon, sire," Selwyn said, "to reach Everyman with the pardon. The Castle of Resistance was on high alert, and the guards were waiting for us. It was quite a battle, but we were victorious in the name of our King. But then when we reached the Dungeon of Condemnation, Everyman rejected the pardon again."

Gilda looked up without touching her food. "We tried, sire, we really did. We offered King Emmanuel's pardon to Everyman again, but he just laughed and said that he was innocent and didn't need the pardon. And then the guards came and took him away, and he thought that he was being released. But then we heard a scream, and..." She buried her face in her hands. "It was terrible! Just terrible!"

Sir Wisdom touched her shoulder. "Aye, Gilda, I know."

She raised a tearstained face to look at him. "We tried so hard to deliver the King's pardon, sire, but he just wouldn't take it." Sobs racked her slender body.

"We failed, sire," Josiah said miserably. "This was our first real mission for His Majesty, and look how it turned out. We failed! Everyman is dead."

"Josiah, Josiah," the old man said gently. "You did not fail, my son. You did exactly as your King required— you delivered King Emmanuel's pardon to Everyman. I can tell by your countenances and your emotions right now that you delivered it with concern and compassion. Aye, Josiah, your mission was a success, for you obeyed your King and followed his instructions completely."

"But we wanted Everyman to accept the pardon. We wanted him to accept King Emmanuel's forgiveness. We wanted him to live!"

"King Emmanuel wanted Everyman to live. But Everyman chose to reject the King's pardon, and in so doing, chose death." The old man put his arms around the three dejected young ambassadors and drew them close to himself. "Gilda, Selwyn, Josiah, hear me. You have obeyed your King. You have delivered his message of forgiveness and attempted to persuade Everyman to accept the pardon. You have done what your King required, and therefore, your mission was a success. The decision to receive or to reject was Everyman's, and he made the wrong decision. That wrong decision is his responsibility, not yours."

Gilda wiped tears from her eyes.

Josiah took a deep breath. "So what do we do now? Go back to the Castle of Faith?"

"Aye," the old man replied, with a twinkle in his eye, "but there is one more assignment that King Emmanuel would have you complete for him before you return to the Castle of Faith."

"What is it?" all three chorused eagerly.

"Remember the Dungeon of Condemnation where you helped free Nathaniel Everyman and his wife? On your way back to the Castle of Faith, pass by that dungeon and deliver pardons to the prisoners languishing there. Within the pages of your book you'll find pardons for everyone. Simply deliver them to any and all who will receive them."

"Will Captain Exclusion oppose us?" Selwyn asked.

"Aye, plan on it," the old man replied. "But you now know how to overcome him. Many of the prisoners in the dungeon will receive the pardons at your hand; some will not. Your task is simply to deliver the message of forgiveness and present King Emmanuel's pardon to any who will receive it."

A thrill of excitement swept over Josiah's soul. "I can't wait to get started," he exclaimed. "Remember that little girl in the dungeon? I know that she will receive a pardon. We can set her free! Remember the old woman who reached out to us so pitifully? She'll listen to us. And there were so many, many others—let's start right away!"

Sir Wisdom smiled. "Get some rest tonight, my young friends. Tomorrow morning we'll call the lepidopteras and they will carry you swiftly to the Dungeon of Condemnation where you shall honor the name of your King by delivering his pardon to the prisoners."

Gilda's eyes sparkled with anticipation. "I can hardly wait!"

Glossary

Bailey: the courtyard in a castle.

Barbican: the space or courtyard between the inner and outer walls of a castle.

Battlement: on castle walls, a parapet with openings behind which archers would shelter when defending the castle.

Castle: a fortified building or complex of buildings, used both for defense and as the residence for the lord of the surrounding land.

Coat of arms: an arrangement of heraldic emblems, usually depicted on a shield or standard, indicating ancestry and position.

Crenel: one of the gaps or open spaces between the merlons of a battlement.

Curtain: the protective wall of a castle.

Doublet: a close-fitting garment worn by men.

Ewer: a pitcher with a wide spout

Furlong: a measurement of distance equal to one-eighth of a mile.

Garrison: a group of soldiers stationed in a castle.

Gatehouse: a fortified structure built over the gateway to a castle.

Great hall: the room in a castle where the meals were served and the main events of the day occurred.

Jerkin: a close-fitting jacket or short coat.

Keep: the main tower or building of a castle.

Lance: a thrusting weapon with a long wooden shaft and a sharp metal point.

Longbow: a hand-drawn wooden bow $5^{1}/_{2}$ to 6 feet tall.

Lute: a stringed musical instrument having a long, fretted neck and a hollow, pear-shaped body.

Lyre: a musical instrument consisting of a sound box with two curving arms carrying a cross bar from which strings are stretched to the sound box.

Merlon: the rising part of a crenallated wall or battlement.

Minstrel: a traveling entertainer who sang and recited poetry.

Moat: a deep, wide ditch surrounding a castle, often filled with water.

Portcullis: a heavy wooden grating covered with iron and suspended on chains above the gateway or any doorway of a castle. The portcullis could be lowered quickly to seal off an entrance if the castle was attacked.

Reeve: an appointed official responsible for the security and welfare of a town or region.

Saboton: pointed shoes made of steel to protect the feet of a knight in battle.

Salet: a protective helmet usually made of steel, worn by knights in combat.

Scullion: a kitchen servant who is assigned menial work

Sentry walk: a platform or walkway around the inside top of a castle curtain used by guards, lookouts and archers defending a castle.

Solar: a private sitting room or bedroom designated for royalty or nobility.

Standard: a long, tapering flag or ensign, as of a king or a nation.

Stone: a British unit of weight equal to fourteen pounds.

Tunic: a loose-fitting, long-sleeved garment.

Trencher: a flat piece of bread on which meat or other food was served.

Castle Facts

- More than 15,000 castles once stretched across Europe and the Near East.
- Castle food was usually spicy, colored with vegetable dyes, and sometimes even gilded with real gold!
- Guests ate with their fingers or with knives or spoons.
- Few people in the Middle Ages knew how to read or write. Schools were few.
- Most people were religious, but since they were unable to read the Bible, they were easily led astray by false churches, which did not teach salvation by faith.
- A knight in armor could be identified by his coat of arms, a colorful design that decorated his shield and his tunic.
- The men who designed coats of arms were called heralds. They made sure that no two designs were the same.
- The designs of the coats of arms were recorded in books called armorials.
- Armor was usually cleaned and polished with sand and vinegar.

Delivering the King's Pardon

Have you ever wished that you could go on a quest for the King—that you could deliver a pardon from King Emmanuel, just as Gilda, Selwyn, and Josiah did? You can, by telling others about the King who wants to pardon them and adopt them into his royal family! His name is Jesus, and he's the King of kings and Lord of lords. If you are a child of the King, he wants you to tell others about him. The message that you need to share with others is as simple as A-B-C:

Admit that you are a sinner. The Bible tells us: *"For all have sinned, and come short of the glory of God." (Romans 3:23)* Every one of us have done wrong things and sinned against God. Our sin will keep us from heaven and condemn us to hell. We need to be forgiven.

Believe that Jesus died for you. The Bible says: *"But God commendeth his love toward us, in that, while we were yet sinners, Christ died for us." (Romans 5:8)* The King of kings, the Lord Jesus Christ, became a man and died for our sins on the cross, shedding his blood for us so that we can be forgiven. Three days later, he arose from the grave.

Call on Jesus to save you. The Bible says: *"For whosoever shall call upon the name of the Lord shall be saved." (Romans 10:13)* Admit to God that you are a sinner. Believe that Jesus died for you on the cross and then came back to life in three days. Call on Jesus in faith and ask him to save you. He will! And when he saves you from your sin, he adopts you into his wonderful family. You become a child of the King!

(Note: If you've never received Jesus as your own King and been adopted into the Royal Family, read the ABC message above and do it right now! And then, after you have become a child of the King, begin telling others how they can do it, too!)